Throw-Away Faces

A Novel by

Josef Alton

To Kerry and John,
I hope you enjoy this
little book. Thanks for
Everything!
        Best
        Josef Alton

ISBN: 978-1-68433-200-7
PUBLISHED BY BLACK ROSE WRITING
www.blackrosewriting.com

Printed in the United States of America
Suggested Retail Price (SRP) $18.95

Throw-Away Faces is printed in Palatino Linotype

Praise for

Throw-Away Faces

"A gritty novel that weaves its way through the backstreets of Seattle and Dublin; Alton has crafted a pacy and sophisticated transatlantic thriller set to the tune of history."
  -*Dr.* Conor Mulvagh, Lecturer in Modern Irish History, UCD

"I want to hold the written pages and embrace the richness of detail and characters and taste the settings so lovingly established by the author. The reader is treated to samples of Scotland, Ireland and Seattle and the imagination of this writer delivers in spades. Enjoy it, live it, love it."
  -Robert E. Kearns, author of *Hy Brasil: Island of Eternity*

"Josef Alton honors the history of Seattle even as he bends it to serve his engrossing, and deeply intriguing tale of murder and municipal malfeasance. Enoch Campbell may be a fiction, but he lives and breathes in these pages and now in my imagination as I pass by Yesler Way."
  -Mark Baumgarten, author of *Love Rock Revolution*

for Jane

Author's Note

At the back of this novel are endnotes which are meant to be read alongside the main text. However, I will leave the reading of these historical digressions entirely up to you.

Throw-Away Faces

"All for ourselves, and nothing for other people, seems, in every age of the world, to have been the vile maxim of the masters of mankind."
—*Adam Smith, Wealth of Nations*

"The attendance of that brother was now become like the attendance of a demon on some devoted being that had sold himself to destruction"
—*James Hogg, The Private Memoirs and Confessions of a Justified Sinner*

"For neither life nor nature cares if justice is ever done or not."
—*Patricia Highsmith*

Prologue

Dear Doctor Dooley,

You will not remember me, but you tended to a friend of mine who died many years ago. At the time when we met outside Glasgow I had no idea we would be linked through a common fate, death following us wherever we settled. Unlike you, I did not choose an occupation waged inside the crypt; I became a lawyer. As I write I am aware of the irony entangled within my words, and I will leave it for you to ponder. I will say, however, it was not the opacity, rigidity or even the aridity of the law that deadened my heart, but rather its miscarriage, and further still a disturbed individual who waged an ill-conceived crusade against a miscarriage of justice through an evocation of evil.

It is not my intention within this letter to explain the details of my ill-fated journey into the forests of the American frontier. Rather, I tracked you down some years back to find you long since departed for Ireland and I let the case rest. It was not until last week that I picked up the newspaper and read about the strange patricides taking place in Dublin and their disturbing similarity to the murders I experienced in Seattle when I was a young man.

I have spent the past few days writing furiously to reconstruct the events of June 1889 in Seattle, as I saw them. I know of no one else in Dublin, and I am sure, based on your standing as a doctor, that you have the proper friends to contact if this manuscript moves you and perhaps compels you to inform the Royal Irish Constabulary of the innocence of the girls suspected of murdering their fathers, and also the resurrection of a killer. I leave this manuscript with you in good faith, as I left my friend in your care many years before. Let us pray for a more positive result than the conclusion to our first meeting those many years ago.

Your servant,
Enoch Campbell

I had the dream again. She's there, sitting on a rock, looking out to sea and I'm looking at her, then she falls. Well, half of her falls. An apparition of her sits up from her own seated body and slips off the cliff. I jump up and look over the side, horrified, and I see her body flail and her white dress whip with the wind as she gets smaller and smaller until she disappears into the black swell of the Irish Sea. Her other body comes up behind me, caresses my back and then pushes me off the cliff. In mid-flight, when the air is being sucked from my lungs, a rigorous pounding shakes me awake.

I opened my eyes and the death of the night hummed in my ears, and I lay there thinking I drowned until the pounding returned and the shadow of two feet laid planted and interrupting the slit of light which glowed on the other side of my hotel-room door.

"Enoch," Madame Lou Graham[i] said, "it's happened again."

I sat up and asked myself two questions. The horrible dream I couldn't seem to burn, yes it would never die. Secondly, where am I? The here-and-now repositioned back into focus. I was in bed, it was late, but telling from the noise downstairs the bar was still open. The killer claimed a new victim. I tore out of bed, shirtless, but in trousers. Halfway to the door, the whisky I consumed earlier drained from my head and into my blood. I made for the door, lost my balance on the way, but grasped the door handle just in time to save myself from falling over.

"Open the door," Lou shouted.

I exhaled and opened the portal to the light. It was blinding, and the short wide woman sutured tight in an armor of imported textiles and feathers stood an inch in front of me. I closed my eyes to avoid straining to focus on her painted face while my eyes adjusted. Her perfume overwhelmed my nose, and I thought I might vomit.

"You reek of poor decisions." She pushed me back into my room and shut the door. "It's happened again," she repeated. "Get dressed."

Lou built this brothel up from the ground and was kind enough to rent out a room to me when three weeks ago there became some confusion concerning my original accommodation. She was heavy, German, and quite awful. However, she was shrewd and sharp as a razor's edge. She was a dangerous opponent—you could tell—and had a big mouth too, which worked to the detriment of all. Despite that, there was a soft side, somewhere. Her tender moments were few and far between, but at least genuine when they surfaced.

"What has happened?" I asked already knowing the answer, "And, how's it you know?"

"I killed the bastard myself, that's how I know." She slapped her palms against her big hips and scowled at me. "A young cop came in and said there's a commotion in the alleyway behind the Oddfellows Hall on Front Street.[ii] He said there's a body face down in the muck."

"And what business is this of mine?"

"What's it to you? You know damn well. You're a witness and the only person the killer communicates with. It has everything to do with you."

Lou swayed as though uncertain whether to turn right or left before twirling towards my sorry excuse for a bed. She sat down, crossed her legs and pulled a cigar from her corset and stared at me like I was supposed to do something. I took the last candle from the fireplace mantle and stood over her as she lit up. She really was as wide as she was tall, black curly hair, and smoked as much as any card playing Yank I'd ever met.

"You know, when I was a girl in Germany," she began, "I used to watch my father smoke in the fields, and I always thought it made him stronger because he worked such long hours." She blew out a thick pillow of smoke and continued. "But, when I got older I realized you don't make nothing by just working hard, you have to use your head. I'd like to think he was smart, but no. He just thought working harder would get him more. The poor man died with a broken body and nothing to show for it. I think about my father every time I smoke in my business—memories don't fade like smoke, but that's beside the point."

"They don't," I said.

"Don't what?"

"Fade. Memories like that."

I was dressed. Lou continued with her poetic thoughts, which she always unleashed after a healthy dram or two of rye. However, they descended into her favorite rant about how she made her fortune.

"How is it you keep the ship afloat?" I said, to keep her ego intact.

"I sit, honey, and watch the wallets come and go as they please."

"Ni bad."

"Surely no, sex is sex. It's the same as any enterprise of sustenance; people need to please their appetite, or run around malnourished and anxious."

"The Church of Scotland would differ," I said. "Now, why am I out of bed again? My head's pounding."

"You've got a killer who needs you," Lou said while another plume of smoke seeped out from between her lips and caressed her round painted cheeks. "Seems the big boys in town think you've bonded with him, or her. Better show your face; you love it anyway. Seems sick to me, but what do I know about you English and your vanity."

"Scottish, Lou. I'm Scottish. Far from an Englishman. There's no vanity up north, just an old Roman wall, some mountains and a ubiquitous sewage problem."

"Besides the fact I can only understand half the things you say, I don't see much difference between the people on your island."

"Ye faschious German, I mi' as weel call ye an Austrian from no on."

"Don't you even think of it!" she thundered, but then smiled, "Faschious?" She queried, "Is that a Scottish word? Your accent always grows thicker when you're upset."

"How I wish I had your friends," I said, ignoring the rest.

"There're no friends in Seattle, just business relationships, deep pockets and vices begging to be filled."

"How lonely," I said.

She smoked looking proud.

"Go on and get out of here. I'm betting the killer left you something," she said.

"What, another letter? Not once on the same day and never at the scene."

"But things are growing more severe, can't you feel it?" she said. "It started with that dead strumpet, but then a respected man. Who's next? I can feel things are getting worse."

I didn't know how to take what she said so I scowled.

"Can you?" I said.

"Oh yes, Lou Graham knows about appetites, and the killer's evil is insatiable."

"And?"

"And the killer wants you to know it. He isn't writing love letters to anyone else. When do you reckon writing will no longer be enough for her? She's going to show you things, Enoch."

"Bloody hell, what's it going to be, a he or she?"

"Both for now until we know for sure, but I hope it's a woman," she said.

"Why?"

"You men have all the fun and have had enough."

Lou sat back satisfied, and I headed to the door not interested in humoring her any longer.

"Lock up, will you?" I asked, turning around halfway to the door. She was still sitting on my bed, picking at my bedspread like she figured out something important in her head. She looked up.

"And what makes you think you're coming back tonight, huh?" she said, cracking a smile. "Oh, my innocent boy of the brothel."

I shook my head, "Not innocent," I said, then turned and left.

I reached the bottom of the stairwell and saw the millionaire, Henry Yesler[iii] conversing with a small group of well-dressed gentlemen. Beside him stood Thomas Burke.[iv] He made eye contact with me, excused himself and approached.

"You're the young Scottish gentleman I've heard about?" he said, holding out his hand.

"I fear you've heard something bad," I said.

"The contrary. My father-in-law is John McGilvra[v], your employer if I'm not mistaken?"

"Oh aye, I've been with the firm two weeks and have yet to meet him."

"He's in San Francisco, but will be back in a week's time."

"That's what I've been told," I said.

Burke possessed a well-mannered grin defined enough to fight off his goatee, and eyes as dark as his hair. I could sense behind his civility lay a shrewd and stark personality.

"How are you finding things?" he asked.

"I mean no offense, but I've seen beyond my share of dead bodies since my arrival."

"It's abominable, and I'm very sorry for it. I've been made aware you are helping Police Chief Butterfield with your insights on the matter?"

There was a twinkle in Burke's eye as though he was fishing for something.

"Yes, to what end, I'm not sure. I'm just a witness who's beginning to see the obvious, a pattern."

"And what pattern might that be?" he asked.

"Their faces."

"All bloody I've heard," he said.

"Destroyed more like it, with a hammer."

"Dear god."

Burke's disposition changed, and he appeared to weaken from my words.

"My apologies," I said.

Yesler approached us.

"Is this the boy who bunks with our loose women?" he asked, dawning a dark-toothed grin.

"Enoch Campbell, is it?"

"Yes Sir, Mr. Yesler."

"You know my name?"

"Everyone knows who you are because you announce it wherever you go," Burke joked.

"Don't be rude, Thomas or I'll make sure you never win my lottery."

Yesler laughed, and Burke winced.

"Enoch," Yesler turned his weak old shoulders and grey head away from Burke's red cheeks, "does this murderer have you next on his list? We'd hate to lose you so soon. Colman did promise your father we'd take care of you."

Yesler's question was a thrown pry bar. I sensed he knew about the killer's letters and hoped to catch me not minding my business. That, or I was being paranoid. Either way, he was a cunning old devil.

"I canna tell," I said.

In his last letter, the killer referred to himself and me as brothers, so it was reasonable to guess I was perhaps the safest person in Seattle. Although, on the other hand, there was no doubt our relationship was doomed to sour at some point. I thought it best to avoid mentioning the letters to Yesler, no matter how much he knew, as their existence would draw me closer into the matter, and for some, to the point of complicity.

"Does he not send his friend mail?" Yesler's eyes darkened. "You're not the only one who interests this madman. I'll tell you something, the scantlings which still hang upon those great trees in front of my house won't be removed while I'm alive, no matter who threatens so!"

"I'm sorry Mr. Yesler, but I don't follow," I said, surprised by his sudden fury.

"Those looters during the riots should have hanged from it too, and if the killer thinks he's going to avoid it, he's wrong. This is my city, not his!"[vi]

Yesler's bottom lip trembled, and he looked like he was a step away from either battering me or weeping on my shoulder. He pulled a kerchief from his herringbone topcoat and cleaned the poison from his lips.

Burke interjected, "Henry, Henry, come now, it's water under the bridge, and Enoch here knows nothing of these old Seattle squabbles." He tried to put his arm around Yesler, but Yesler rejected it with a violent turn. "Enoch, please forgive Henry."

"It's an honor to meet you, Mr. Yesler, and I'm sorry if my connection to the killings has offended you."

"It's my nerves," Yesler said.

"These killings have us all anxious," Burke said.

"Aye, they do," I said. "I apologize, but I must be going."

"Speak of the devil, were we not just speaking about the killer? Have you any sense being on the streets alone at night while he's on the prowl?" Yesler said.

"I'm not travelling far."

"It was a pleasure," Burke said, shaking my hand again, "I will see you at the firm. My start in Seattle was under McGilvra. I hope you learn as much as I did from the experience."

"If I learn half as much I will consider myself a lucky man," I said.

Burke smiled and came in closer. "Today's paper should answer any lingering questions you might have about Henry's mood." He handed me a rolled-up newspaper. I begged Yesler goodbye, and he hacked and drew his handkerchief back to his mouth.

"A pleasure meeting you both," I said.

Yesler half waved while he tended to his recovery.

Nearing the door, I saw one of Lou's girls I'd never seen before speaking to another young gentleman. She turned and eyed me. I felt embarrassed and turned away. Memories from my old life raged back, and I hurried outside.

•   •   •   •   •

I stepped out of Lou's and dodged a group of drunkards on the boardwalk.

"Watch where you're going," one said, while the others laughed. I unrolled the newspaper Burke gave me and read the headlines. "Months later, still no sign of the Ripper in Whitechapel." Beside that read, "Anonymous Letter to Yesler: 'I'm going to steal your scantlings.'" This explained Yesler's mood. My interest was piqued; I opened the paper and continued to read not worrying about the body up the street.

"Police Chief Butterfield acknowledged an anonymous letter was sent to politician and businessman, Henry Yesler, stating his scantlings—made famous in the 1882 mob lynching of two murderers and one suspected murderer—will be stolen from the trees where the men were hanged without trial. The scantlings have stayed lodged in the trees for the past seven years.

"Yesler refused to comment, but Butterfield admitted the millionaire who owns the property where the lynching took place, and who publicly agreed with the tragic miscarriage of law and public order, was agitated by the letter and attributed it to the killer who has claimed two victims in the past three weeks. The lynching, which brought national indignation upon Seattle, is still considered by many the main reason why Northern Pacific Railroad chose rival city, Tacoma as its main terminus of the Northwestern region.[vii] A sore spot which has left business leaders interested in a main railroad line between Seattle and other major American cities, smarting.[viii]

"Yesler's own troubles in regard to the old city lottery scarred his reputation.[ix] Guilty of fraud in 1876, Yesler was found to have abused lottery funds and contributed to the spike in criminal activity which corresponded to the popularity of the lottery and influx of criminality. The murders and the subsequent mob lynching were the apex of the city's trouble with criminal disorder. Seattle's wave of crime as of late has reopened old wounds which Yesler and Seattle's old citizens wish were healed.

"As of yet there are no leads to the killer's identity, and Butterfield suggests every citizen be on their guard until the killer is brought to justice."

I let the paper slip out from my hands and onto the glaur of the street.

I turned into the alleyway and onto the crime scene.

"What took you so long?" Police Chief Butterfield said.[x] He pulled me out from the small crowd of onlookers. "I've got half the mind to make you the prime suspect considering how often you're at the scene before I send an officer to collect you."

"You didn't send someone?" I said. "Lou woke me up to say one of yours rang to do just that."

Butterfield flashed me an angry look.

"I'll want to talk to her about this visitor tomorrow," he said.

"I'm sure she'll more than be obliged to fulfill your request," I said.

Butterfield snorted from his bulbous nose as if to expel the scent of his distaste for Madame Lou. He looked back to me and nodded; the nod I understood to communicate if I was ready to view the body and see if it triggered any memories from the first killing.

"I still want to look at the letter he sent you," Butterfield said.

"I'll see if I can find it, I think I may have thrown it away," I lied and for no good reason other than I wanted to keep the letter and I didn't see what good it would do to hand it over.

"It was typed anyway," I lied again. "Not much you can study from it."

He seemed unpleased and turned to the crime.

"Now, I want you to look around and mind if you see anything peculiar," he said. "Anything that might jog your memory."

"Peculiar? I suppose, besides the body of a man or woman?"

"This one's a little different," he said.

"Than a man or lassie?"

I scanned Butterfield's face, up from his thick creamy mustache to his small Norwegian eyes, and in the dark, saw the blue fires within them were ablaze with fear. Real fear. My stomach tightened.

"A lass, again?" I asked.

"No."

Butterfield grabbed my arm and led me to the body. The alley opened up. The sides of the wooden buildings which encased the alley floor stood opaque enough to create a sort of slatted projector screen. The policemen's lanterns cast us as long green shadows against them.

In the very middle of this picture show lay a doll. It lay face down in the muck, the frills of its little dress still white like snow. But this was no doll, and Butterfield was right; the victim was not a woman, but a little girl.

I looked away, and again to the alley's wooden sides, watching the elongated bodies of chief Butterfield's lantern holders tower over me, and I could have sworn I entered a satanic ritual. I walked closer to the child. She lay prostrate, her arms straight at her sides, both palms facing up and open to the godless stars. Her feet were fixed and her toes sunken into the mud. Her face was pushed deep into the mud with plenty of blood pooled around her splayed golden locks, enough so her head looked like a buried meteorite cooling in the earth. There was no doubt he placed her like this. My thoughts started to race.

"Who else has broken the perimeter past her feet?" I asked.

"The perimeter?"

"Who has walked beyond her feet to investigate the body?"

"Myself, and you," he said in a worried tone.

I touched her arm, and it was cold like meat in the icebox. I inspected for footprints in the mud and found mine and Butterfield's. However, there was another set, straight towards the girl, then a confused storm surrounding the victim, and a line out towards the street. I noticed the bottom of the girl's bare feet. Clean.

"She was killed somewhere else," I said. "Look at the tracks leading in and out of the alley. Her feet are clean. She was positioned to lay like this."

Butterfield wrinkled his face as if the girl was over-peppered and he needed to sneeze. The information appeared to destroy his prior benchmark for the breadth of depravity. He judged the murder in religious terms; within a holy plexus of every sin ever committed he filed the girl's remains under "most evil."

"But where could she have been killed," he responded after a moment to collect himself.

My vision of the crime appeared. A father watched. One at a time. The youngest child to the eldest. No mother. Why no mother? The father got it last. Jaw breaking, skull fragments, blood on cedar. Kitchen floor. Finished, the killer carries the girl's body out into the cold, wrapped in a canvas drape, taking her away from all the pain. It was a sacrifice, and a mercy killing, she's an unwilling martyr for something.

"Where?" Butterfield repeated.

"I don't know. A house, more victims, the entire family? Have there been complaints of a missing child?"

"No, and couldn't be; multiple victims, it doesn't follow the pattern."

He was right. It didn't follow the pattern, but it felt right. Lou said something was changing, and I felt it too.

"Anything else?" I didn't answer. He continued, "Well, what if we have another killer now? There's enough drunk and angry Indians and Chinese in this town for more than one to crack and kill a child."

I didn't listen. I knew it was the same killer. It felt right—found at night, the body belly-down, sunken in the mud, her face—I turned back to the poor girl, and it hit me. Her face. I turned to Butterfield, but he walked back into the small crowd of curious onlookers. His officers remained, standing shoulder-to-shoulder, looking at me with their tin lanterns propped up against their chests. They stared at me like they hated me. As if, since I was the closest to the body, I was the one to blame. Blame the foreigner. I rushed past them. Butterfield tried without success to make the crowd, the vampires of the city, go away.

I abandoned the girl and the lantern guard and ran off screen.

"Chief," I grabbed his arm, "I think something might've been placed under her face."

He swung around and lost his hat.

"What?"

The lanterns shifted behind me and illuminated us.

"We need to lift her."

He saw the excitement in my eyes and frowned. I felt guilty."

"We need to wait," he said.

"Of course, for the doctor," I said.

•　　　•　　　•　　　•　　　•

We waited, for what seemed to me like half-an-hour. Then, like a black cat, Dr. Tom sauntered into the alleyway. His doctor's bag clapped against the side of his short leg. He was a small man and his black bowler and heavy overcoat looked like steel garments swaddling a child. A dainty pair of wire-rimmed spectacles slipped from his nose, a nothing nose, not more than a bump. He was pale and diaphoretic. He stepped to Butterfield with his lips pursed, stapled and stitched. He nodded to me, but walked right past and breached the line of lantern holders like a ghost gliding past their broad shoulders without them turning to notice. A local. He stood over the girl and inspected her body, as still as a statue. I was at a loss to recite any known incantation of resurrection that could lift her up from the alley's midnight gravity and give the doctor his miracle. Butterfield and I walked up and stood beside him.

"She's dead," Dr. Tom said.

Their shadows stretched stupid against the alley wall as they made small talk of the killings.

Their conversation continued, and panic filled my chest. I couldn't tolerate them discussing the gruesome nature of the crimes. I felt the flames erupt in me. A horrible brushfire of anxiety spread through my body, wanting out up through my mouth. Whatever was under the poor girl's face called to me. I was never the practitioner of the occult, but the evil atmosphere in the alleyway made it hard to breathe. Some devil was close by casting spells on us, putting strange thoughts in our heads — at least in my own.

"May we turn her, doctor?" I interrupted.

Butterfield nodded and Dr. Tom said, "Yes, but I hope to God you don't find what you're looking for." I nodded back to them and imagined the girl's teeth plugged into the muck and situated like a Celtic stone circle in the middle of some enchanted nowhere in the Highlands. An archaic looking aristocratic man stood in the middle of it, wearing a powdered wig and a torn face. The macabre image of the distorted Robespierre[xi], disintegrated. Now, it was my hand, severed from my body, laying inside her mouth.

"I will need to be the one who turns the body," the doctor grimaced.

"I hope to God you don't find what you're looking for—" The doctor's words repeated in my head. What am I looking for? I asked myself. *"I hope you don't find what you're looking for—"* Perhaps, it'll find me—maybe it already has. I'm lost.

The doctor set down his bag and knelt beside her, and I on the other side. He pulled her up, and she was caked with mud, her face a blank of molten chocolate and strawberry jam. There was no nose, no eyes, no mouth, her identity was erased. I couldn't look for more than a second. It was too grotesque. I diverted my eyes to the crater where her head was, but there was nothing there either.

I felt the rain lick the back of my neck. I closed my eyes and listened to my breathing. I felt ashamed. I imagined Butterfield and the doctor eyeing at each other with the braided feeling of mutual relief and disdain for me. I wanted to open my eyes again and for there to be, mixed in with the mud, what I hoped to find—but still nothing, just a pool of blood. Butterfield knelt with us. I felt like he wanted me to say something profound in order to have the killing make sense, but I was speechless.

Moving amongst the layers of silence above, an amorphous blank descended from the sky and crashed to the ground beside us. Butterfield leapt on the doctor's back, sending them both across the girl's body and straight onto me. I fell flat with them on top.

The weight of the men pressed the air out of my lungs, and I pushed them off my chest in a furious rage. Butterfield raised his arm to strike me, but the parcel that was dropped from the heavens took precedence, and he turned to see the naked body of a man, arms splintered and broken, his right leg bent backwards, his torso contorted, his face hammered in to the point the splintered stubs of what used to be his jaw were all that remained. Tied around the corpse's neck hung a silver amulet. Cigar burns enveloped his chest.

The Doctor stood up, backed away and removed a box from within his inside coat pocket. Shaking, he opened it and pushed whatever powder it contained up his nose. I imagined the girl I saw at Lou's stripped naked and lying dead upon my mattress. I was smoking a cigar and ghosts came out from my mouth. These evil testaments pronounced themselves and with such ease they felt ordinary, and their collective significance did not exceed the reach of fact. They were banal truths that were bound to exist if not to repeat themselves, and this I took to mean I was seeing the normal passage of time, but in a twisted other world—in a lawless America.

Butterfield repeated, "oh God" again and again, and the rhythm of his hysteria counted off the steps of the dancing demons who pranced within the sheaths of lantern light which beat off the chest of the girl's father. The aristocrat in the center of the Celtic circle made of the little girl's teeth reappeared in my mind, and he took off his charred visage to reveal a single word: purity. We were in his world now, and no one was allowed to leave his circle.

Ⅰⅰ

The afternoon sun lanced through my father's study windows in golden dust-laden bars. We had not spoken in quite some time, but for the past few weeks, I knew this meeting was coming, and I dreaded its arrival. He sat behind his desk in a large padded desk chair and I in a smaller rendition of the same, minus the armrests. His private study was filled with the volumes of intellectual masterworks written by Scotland's greatest minds. He was an engineer by schooling but was a businessman more than anything else. He said he was a man of common sense and reason. I presumed this accounted for his often cold and reserved manner in which he approached fatherhood.

He stared at me without expression until the right side of his face twitched. It was curious because his battle to control the curl of his upper lip continued in spite of the fact his mustache was itchy and simply needed a scratch. Father was a proud man, and I suppose he thought if he were to break his stare to relieve an itch it would undermine the connotation of his scolding. I smiled, and he cleared his throat and covered his mouth with a fist pressed tight to his upper lip.

"You are still in a state?"

"What does that mean?" I asked.

"You haven't recovered."

"I don't know father, should I be?"

"It was the worst thing, and I would never wish it on anyone, let alone my own son, but there is much to be said for moving forward. After all, if you don't let go, you get dragged along the road."

Our Glasgow house stood tall and peered down on the extravagance of the botanical gardens on the eastern end of Byres Road.

An uncompromising edifice, the house was a yellow cliff of ashlar blocks. Dad loved her, even though she was cold, and named her Bessy, which I thought odd, but everyone else found it endearing.

"It has been two years since your studies were completed and a year since your internship ended. You are a competent advocate and should continue your work," he said.

"Have you talked to mother lately?" I asked.

"She's not talking."

"She talks to me."

"That is not talking; that's her sickness."

"It's her," I said.

"Do not think that I'm unconscious of your attempt to change the subject. I'm not interested in your mother right now; you and your competence is what I aim to discuss."

"I'm fine," I said.

"You are not fine, Enoch."

"I'm becoming fine, father."

"You are becoming an appendage to your mattress."

I laughed.

"I suppose you're right."

"Do you mind James Colman?"

"Colman? They stayed here when I was a boy, did they not?"

"He was a friend from university who flitted to America."

"I suppose I do mind of him, but why?"

"He has offered to act as your benefactor and I agreed. You will travel to the City of Seattle in America to continue your legal profession and to spread our business interests to that market depending on how you settle."

"You cannot do this; I wish to stay."

"As you are an adult I would in normal circumstances never force you into a decision, but it's my opinion you are in no clear state of mind to take care of yourself, as you have shown by the scar you have left upon your right wrist."

"But to send me to the other side of the world?" I said.

"You need a new world to explore, lad; you're cannibalizing

yourself."

"I'm not mad, or mother—it will take time."

"How long?" he yelled. I started in my seat. "Six more months, six years! Ni, I canna lose you too. I'd rather it this way and hope an adventure will sort you oot. Time seems a thin bandage for your scenario."

I was speechless. A stranger to the world—a stranger to myself and to my former life. How long would it take to recover if I stayed in Glasgow? I was bored there; it was full of crumbling moss-eaten churches and rough street stalkers looking for a bowler hat to flick off your head and land in a puddle. I would be safer in Seattle and could perhaps stop running.

·   ·   ·   ·   ·

I jumped over the body of the splintered man and looked up to the rooftops above. A silhouette stood on the edge of the building looking down at his good work. He then ran along its ledge, turning in and out of view. There were two ways out of the alley—north or south. I elected to trot south towards Skid Road[xii] and into the Lava Beds.[xiii]

"Where the hell do you think you're going?" Butterfield yelled.

I turned back and saw his shadow backlit by his men's lanterns. "I'm running south. You go north," I yelled back. The lanterns boggled then turned out of sight, and with them, Butterfield. Through the muck I sprinted to the mouth of the alley and stopped facing the fire station on Columbia Street.[xiv] It stood out as if it were embossed with some twinkle of significance I was yet to understand. Then, looking left, into the dead of the streets, the silhouette of long arms and outstretched legs flew across the street. There he was.

I ran up the street and connected with his path and turned south onto 2nd Avenue, in pursuit. The streets were nearly empty. Random nightwalkers shivered with the gaslight reflecting off the lines of stagnant puddles collected inside the wheel ruts of the street. The killer's athleticism: his mechanical gait sent the staggering bodies against the walls of the decaying wooden buildings, and I was losing him. The poison from the drink and cigars I consumed earlier in the night broke from their slumber and injected new violence into my bloodstream. I felt I was going to faint, but I needed to keep going and run faster. I needed to concentrate.

He turned right. I passed the St. Charles Hotel[xv] and turned with him onto Cherry Street. Yesler's Hall stood like an arrogant idiot on Front Street. Without the lanterns, I couldn't see the shadow any longer. He evaporated. I guessed left and pushed south on Front and then he appeared out of a doorway and stood in the distance looking back at me. He turned and continued, hovering over the softness of the street. But I was beginning to warm up, I could feel the gears in my legs loosen and I coughed out the needles in my lungs and surged into a sprint down the block to its end. He veered right at the Throat[xvi], near the Triangle Block. Our trajectories were linked and I was gaining on him now. Together we shot passed Washington Street and I felt the tug of the rope as he cut off the open street and into the entrance of the Brunswick Hotel.[xvii]

I pushed through the front doors and the garden pattern of the foyer's long carpet came alive and the dahlias bloomed at my feet and her ivy stalks snaked up my legs as I stopped in a huff of panic. "Where?" I yelled to the gloomy skeleton-key-shaped concierge. Without a word, he pointed to the end of the hallway and grinned. I ripped free from the stalks and came to the end of the hall. There, to the right was a pine and burned-oil scented bar manned by a barkeep building a glass pyramid of snifters on top of the bar's cool slate. Could it be the concierge and the barkeep were the same man? For, they appeared the same, pointed the same and administered the same seditious smirk.

I punched through the back door and into the alley. Facing me was a Chinese laundry. A red lamp hummed blood in a window beside a wooden door dog-eared ajar. I entered and the weight of the darkness inside pressed on me. The quiet set in. The smell of detergent and starch mixed with the smell of incense. My heavy breath shook the walls covered with hanging wool coats and shimmering silk garments. My eyes were slow to adjust, as if they were not meant to, as if I didn't belong there. In this house, I stuttered in the dark like a foreigner. Tapestries of kanji script pushed out from the hallway walls I stumbled between to impress upon me I was perhaps approaching a final act; that this race was to soon come to a sinister conclusion. I reached another door, back out into the cold night, and onto a laundry platform subjugated with sheets hung from wash lines.

"The moon is out," The devil said, "how many days has it been since the last time?"

The soft voice knocked me back on my heels and the door slammed behind me, and then a shadow blazed past. My blood solidified into mortar. I was bricked in, afraid; I chased fear into a room of mirrors, of white screens of which echoed the alleyway where this nightmare began. The moon indeed was out, showing through a crack between the smoky clouds overhead. All was still besides the sheets rippling with the breeze.

"What brings a Scotsman to such an unfortunate place? Could it be for love or money? Have the English taken your wild spirits and made you theirs?"

I hadn't the faintest idea what he was on about. However, my warm blood told me he was wrong; I wanted his life all of a sudden and nothing more.

"What do you know of it?" I said.

"What do we know of wherever we are from?"

The ghost's silhouette appeared amongst the sheeted lines; taller and thinner from the casted projection.

"Perhaps this is not the most opportune moment to traverse Smith's social theory, but do you not see yourself living in another time now that your soul is again housed within the wilderness?"

"Not all Scotsmen are philosophers."

"No, but the death of culture is a preoccupation you carry like a stain on your pressed collars, is it not? But, enough of that!"

The sheet broke, and the killer charged through the rest, landing his shoulder into my chest with such force I was lifted from my feet and sent back a yard, cracking the back of my head against the ground. I opened my eyes and I expected him to be standing over me and reveal his identity before ending me. Instead, he was gone. I gasped for air, and tried to stand, but staggered and fell back to my seat. Again, he spoke.

"However, I'm happy you came," he said, "and you came right when I figured out my place in this town. Right when I realized where my place was in this miasma of social disunity. I find so much religion in this broken experiment."

He spoke nonsense, but with such clarity, I could not help but be somewhat captivated by his words; they spun against the linens like good American verse, and indeed perhaps he was an artist, I thought. But the thought made me feel strange enough for my fear to return.

"Kill me if you're going to do it," I said.

"I don't believe in suicide without principle and nor should you.

"Then I'll kill you instead."

"A redundancy," he said. "Let's not talk in circles. Why not cultivate our gifts amongst the deaths of others; isn't that a more constructive mode of expression?"

I heard a crash—what sounded like a door being kicked in—and the warmth of the devil withdrew from my body, and he was gone. I stood and forced myself to ignore the pain in my chest and at the back of my head to continue the chase. I still felt the connection—the tug of the rope tied around our respective waists pulled us through another Chinese laundry like weightless spirits. I ended out the other side and onto what must have been 2nd Avenue. He stood waiting in the middle of the road adjacent to the Standard Theater. He was still and black as a stencil—his long coat growing a popped collar into a murderous crown. I knew not why I was still chasing him; maybe out of boredom or out of a deep desire to die tonight. However, his nature was belligerently gallus[xviii] and injected a drop of hate into my blood. I wanted revenge. There would be no more philosophy tonight.

He continued south and turned right on Main Street, back towards Elliott Bay, and when he hit Commercial Street he took another right, passing the New England Hotel and the Brunswick, which we already entered. When I passed the hotel, the same miserable concierge was standing behind the hotel's front glass door, watching me give chase, and I suspected with the same chilling smile he administered minutes before.

We circled the block and I felt the killer was leading me somewhere. I was growing weary, but I couldn't slow myself. Ahead, he turned left onto Washington Street, and onto the docks. I reached the corner and saw his ghost standing under a large sign. He vanished inside the Langston Livery Stable.[xix] I entered through a crack in the livery's massive rollaway door and almost cut myself on the sharp flashing which ran the length of the door's edge.

The livery was pitch black except for a glow emanating from behind a door at the top of the staircase located at the far side of the stable. The odor of hay and horseshit pricked the inside of my nose like I consumed a spoonful of hot mustard. It was here my anger subsided and I realized I was in grave danger. My choices were few, I could run away and save myself, put my back against a wall and wait until my eyes adjusted, or, walk into the darkness as if blindfolded and stage the beginning of my own death. I took two steps forward, into the nothingness, and just when I knew my time was up, my path was cut short by a large funeral coach. Smacking my head against its side, I then stepped through the spokes of its back wheel and fell to the ground in a heap. So much for my dramatic entrance into hell, I thought. I heard the killer laugh across the livery, and I wondered if he was nocturnal.

His voice bounced off the livery's naked rafters.

"I meant to tell you, a coach was not far from the entrance," he said.

I lay there, shaking off the ache, and felt my body sink into the wet earth. My eyes adjusted to the dark, and beside me a mess of horse legs shooting up from the ground like knuckled pillars. I rolled on my stomach and crawled underneath the carriage and into a berth allocated for a single white thoroughbred. She was aware of my presence and gave a vexed snort and stamped. If the killer won't kill me, this bloody horse will, I thought.

I moved along from one berth to the next until the fear of being surprised left me and the false feeling of confidence, which originally beckoned me inside the livery, returned. I wanted to win again. I suppose, I was a bit confused, not able to decide what I needed. Fear hampers control and I was fixed on taking the killer, finding absolution. Hurting him before he hurt me.

I heard his steps splash inside puddles of horse piss. Random bangs and whacks echoed through the stable. He came closer. I needed a better view of the stable and climbed on top of a full-size stagecoach and rose to find the killer standing on another of the same, not more than twenty feet away. He reacted to my appearance, stunned, but recovered and relaxed his back. The both of us struggled to see, and we were ill at easy to make any sudden decisions until our respective surroundings were scanned, recouped and calculated. There was little either of us could do.

"It appears we are at an impasse," the killer said.

"Yes."

"Have you been enjoying my letters?"

"No," I said.

"I don't believe you."

"You know, the police will be here at some point."

"What makes you think they'll track us here?"

"The concierge at the Brunswick saw us pass and turn onto the docks."

"What concierge?" he said.

"What do you mean? When we ran through the hotel."

The killer shrugged his shoulders, but didn't answer. I felt cold.

"Should we call it a night?" he said.

"I don't think so."

"And why? Is it you wish to kill me, or I to kill you?"

I paused, not knowing how to answer.

"Either way."

He sighed.

"I find your apathy troubling."

I laughed.

"Oh, Aye! My apologies for bringing you worry. Your actions on the other hand, I haven't found the least bit disconcerting."

"My actions are just a physical manifestation of what we do to each other every day. Nothing more."

"Like caving in the faces of small children?" I questioned. "Who are 'we' anyway?"

"The world. This Seattle. Those white men, and 'them' Indians."

"And what do we do to each other?"

"Destroy one another," he said.

"I don't give a bollocks about your philosophy."

"You wanted a reason. I neglected in my letters to get into much detail, so I beg your pardon for thinking you'd want an explanation."

"It's not much of a justification."

"I have to disagree with you, but this is not a conversation for the dark."

He leapt from his coach to an open canopy coach beside it and then hopped from its backseat up to another hardtop ten feet from my own. He did so in one flawless motion. His face was covered with a kerchief, and a bowler was pinched low to obscure his forehead. He was a shadow blocking the leaky glow of the staircase stationed across the livery. Angelic almost, he stood inside a soft prison of diffused light. His shape was familiar.

"I don't believe there will be anymore death tonight," he said. "I'm exhausted from earlier; dragging a man's body across town and carrying him up three flights of stairs without being noticed is no easy task."

"And the girl?"

"Yes, I went back for her while her father lay on the roof."

"Why?"

"We've talked already of redundancies, Enoch. Don't you believe there are better and more pressing matters to discuss?"

"I think not," I said.

"What of the city? If you can call this shack-riddled town such a thing?"

"What of it then?"

"Can you not see?" he said.

"What's it I'm supposed to see?"

"YOU are the one working at the law office. YOU are the boy at their beck and call. Can you not see something's wrong? That some conspiracy is afoot?"

"You know where I work—This doesn't frighten me."

"That's not my point!" he shouted. He cooled himself and continued. "Not my point at all. Do the wealthy want to live in wooden homes when there's stone?"

"I've already said enough with your philosophy."

"Don't be an idiot. Think. You yourself must find this place a relic. How do you think the wealthy feel? This ruddy and rotten wooden town is scraping for survival—never forget it."

"Perhaps this isn't a topic to discuss in the dark," I said.

"Perhaps it is, being you seem always in it."

"Am I to listen to suggestions of corruption and conspiracy from a monster like yourself?"

"You're in the company of a man, but come soon, you will be at the mercy of the monsters."

He jumped down from his coach and I heard his steps trail away towards the stable door in which we entered. I jumped from my coach and gave chase, but arriving at the entrance, he was nowhere in sight. I peered out the slit of the sliding stable door and looked east towards Commercial Street. I started to pass through the door when a loud screech filled my ears and out of my peripheral vision I saw the lip of the massive wooden slider close on me. In my panic, I did the most stupid thing and jumped outside the livery. My body passed through the door's threshold, but my right hand lagged behind me. The burning tug at the bottom of my arm was the removal of my hand—sliced clean off.

My face fell into the mud and in a fit of total anguish I opened my mouth to scream, but the scream went back inside my lungs and my mouth welcomed a clod of earth inside it. I wanted to spit my insides out onto the ground.

The killer stepped to me as I writhed in pain. He pushed his boot deep into my chest and pinned me to the ground.

"You see, Enoch, you wanted to be in pain. I have given you your wish, another distraction. From now on, don't question me when I speak to you. I'm not as mad as you take me for. Not as mad as the other Scotsman you work for. It's of some luck you are left-handed, but nonetheless I apologize for the inconvenience I have caused you. No doubt you will have the bosom of Madam Graham to cry into tonight, but I hope you don't. You can always bleed to death here too if you wish. Though, I doubt you will."

He vanished inside the dark streets.

I still felt his foot press me into a shallow grave. I was in such pain I hallucinated. I saw both night and day at the same time sweeping across the sky, and the shadows of the wooden buildings mix with the bookshelves from my father's study, and the ceaseless roll of the Atlantic's waves kiss the glass of my cabin's porthole upon the *Ferdinand*, the schooner which sailed me across. I lay there out of breath having run so hard and for so long. Yet, by the end, I had no idea what I ran for, or what I wanted. The pain disappeared. I couldn't feel anything. Not my legs, arms, or neck. I looked down and saw no hand, and with its absence, no scar. I was alone, dying it felt like, in a rotting city I knew nothing about. I heard the police whistles shriek across town, and as they drew nearer, I knew I would be saved. I would be saved, temporarily, from the chase.

Dublin, 1916

It was the Thursday before Easter, in Dublin. Every shop in the city would later be bustling in preparation for the holiday weekend. Thomas Dooley enjoyed his morning walk to his office; it helped clear his mind. For several nights, he struggled to sleep and last night was the same. He lay awake reviewing his past patients in hopes the exercise might trigger his memory, bring up a face to match a certain name. Dooley rose with the sun in his small, lonely quarter and rang the service bell for tea. As soon as he rang he recalled giving the maid the Thursday to shop for her family who lived in the Liberties. He shaved away the night's sleepless stubble, pulled a pressed shirt from the oversized armoire which towered over his doughy single bed and descended the steps of his flat onto O'Connell Street[xx], his stomach rumbling and full of acid from last night's porter.

He stumped across town, his cane stabbing the footpath, the ping of its ferrule ricocheting off the monolithic columns of the General Post Office.[xxi] He passed the rows of stone structures without paying them much mind for he was used to the buildings of Dublin towering above him. Dooley tapped his cane onto O'Connell Bridge and the sight of the River Liffey slowed his pace. The brown bows of churning water and aggravated sediment ran high and swift towards the belly of Dublin Bay. He watched the miniature whirlpools which formed on the side of the river's steep rock walls drift into the middle of the stream and disappear. The speed of the river reminded him, although a holy day drew near, a thick ribbon of anxiety cut through the hearts of every Dubliner, gashing the city's feast day tranquility. It wasn't religious tension or Fenian agitation, but the bizarre string of patricides that set the city alight with fear. The murders, and the mysterious manuscript dropped on his doorstep the night before last, were what troubled the doctor. A peculiar feeling of doom settled upon his shoulders much like the morning fog clung to the cobbled roads of Temple Bar.[xxii] Who was this Enoch Campbell, and why did he send him this grisly record of murders?

"Thom Dooley, is it?"

Dooley started and turned around.

"Cormac," he said. "You gave me a fright."

"Sorry, doctor. You alright?"

The short, pear-shaped man, with sideburns cut at an angle to resemble bookends, clasped his hands to rest on top of his protruding stomach before throwing them to his sides, and sheathing them inside his trouser pockets.

"How's the paper?" Dooley said.

"Grand, grand."

"You must be keeping the typewriters chiming I imagine?"

Dooley noticed Cormac appeared a wee too warm on such a cool morning. Beads of perspiration held onto the weak strings of his thinning hairline. He pulled a handkerchief from the breast pocket of his jacket and mopped at his face.

"Busy for all the wrong reasons," he said.

"What, with this Republican nonsense?"

"Oh, if it were just the politics the *Times* would be happy," he said. "No, it's these murders in the Liberties."

"Aye?"

"There was another last night," he said. "Another Republican. That makes two of them, and two Unionists to match."

"Unionists[xxiii] in the Liberties?"[xxiv]

"They're there."

Dooley sighed and peered up to the foggy Georgian rooflines which towered above them.

"At this juncture, is it beyond the realm of our imagination to gather a killing in Dublin is not religiously or politically motivated?"

Cormac relaxed his shoulders and let out a hefty laugh.

"That's a point I have failed to consider, just evil without a cause to justify it," he said. "If it were just a matter of hot tempers and drunken brawls I'd have no worry. But four dead fathers, four daughters waking up covered in their father's own blood, and each with a hammer in her hand? Cannot stomach thinking about, no less writing about it."

"A hammer?" Dooley's face blanched.

"You okay there, Thom?"

"And the girls?" Dooley said.

"Tucked away in Kilmainham Gaol, naturally."

"Bollocks to naturally, there's nothing natural to any of it."

"No, sorry, the RIC sent the fourth girl to hospital," Cormac said.

"She was hurt?"

"Mad," he said. His pocked face went flat as a dish. "You wouldn't want to take a trip out to her and see what the doctors are saying would ye?"

"Cormac, I keep my medicine outside politics, and I keep it out of the papers."

"The likes of treating that diluted Fenian, Plunkett[xxv], I cannot dispute the steel of your oath," he said.

"It's a matter of treating the lungs."

"Consumption is above this island's issues, is it?" Cormac said.

"Aye, and getting to the bottom of these murders."

"Are ye proposing the girls are innocent?"

Dooley stared past Cormac and for the first time since the arrival of the strange letter and manuscript, believed whoever this Enoch Campbell was might be telling some truths.

"It could be a lone killer," Dooley said. "He could be smart and cunning. Who's to say a killer canna be intelligent?" He turned back to Cormac. "Or, maybe he's what we all fear here in Ireland, a foreigner, like me!"

"That's right," Cormac laughed.

"Must be on my way to the office."

"And I to my typewriter."

"Now don't quote me on anything, Cormac."

"I heard nothing of interest," Cormac said. "Anyway, I'd never slight a Scotsman—I value my wellbeing too much for that." He smiled and turned on his way.

·   ·   ·   ·   ·

The Royal Irish Academy[xxvi] asked Dr. Dooley several weeks ago to give a talk about the late arrival of consumption to Ireland and his own personal experiences of fighting the disease on the island and abroad. He sat in his dark office which overlooked Dame Street and scowled in the direction of the old parliament building.[xxvii] He didn't possess a single idea how to start his talk. He was supposed to be an authority on the subject, but because more patients died during his career than were saved he felt absurd to talk on the matter. Perhaps, he thought, he should open with an admission of guilt: that in fact he chose to specialize in the treatment of consumption due of his acute fear of failure that established itself as a phobia when he flunked out of the School of Surgeons, in Edinburgh. As he would declare, "You see, when you treat those who cannot be saved you erase the chances of killing a patient, and if on the off chance a patient survives, you as the doctor, will be hailed a hero." His youthful imagination promised him he'd never be held responsible for anyone's death, but as the years have passed by, the more burdensome his guilt. "The drink helps," he'd tell them and they would laugh, misunderstanding his confession as humor.

A dead father, and a bloody girl holding a hammer.

A dead father, and a dead daughter splayed out in a dark alley.

The manuscript. He stood up from his chair and walked over to his satchel hanging from his coat rack and pulled a rectangular parcel wrapped in brown butcher paper from it and set it on his desk. He could see his breath in the cold office. He unwound the waxed cord tethered around it and pinched the first quarter inch of the document he already read and flipped it upside down away from the rest. *IV*, it read at the top.

Dooley didn't remember Enoch. The time when their paths may or may not have crossed was at the height of his melancholy. To his recollection, 1887 or '88 was a time of no quittance. He sighed and stopped ignoring the crystal decanter of sherry on his bookshelf. He read his watch. 10 am, not the earliest he ever poured a drink. He did so and returned his eyes to the manuscript. Cormac's wet lips entered his mind, repeating the word, *hammer*. The tool used in Dublin matched the murders in Seattle, but there's no proof the killers were one in the same.

Enoch himself is off, Dooley thought. The letter alone was odd, and that he played such a minor role in Enoch's life made it disconcerting that he, after all these years, was first to come into the mind of a near stranger. He'd his share of letters from the families of his deceased patients. Though he tried to avoid meeting with them, he could never do so. The awkward introductions, the swollen red eyes and incessant thank-yous were bloody awful, every time. Enoch was something different. The fact he didn't directly write to the RIC was enough for the doctor to distrust his state of mind, not to mention the liberties he took with the manuscript. Enoch's letter said he wrote a reconstruction of what happened in Seattle, but he wrote himself at the centre of the drama. Why on earth, Dooley thought to himself, do I need the particulars of some chase through a city I care nothing about, or what color of brassiere some madam wore on a Wednesday? He finished his glass of sherry. Rain droplets formed on his window and whetted his appetite for another glass.

Lurching forward at the desk, the doctor clasped his hands and pushed his knuckles up against his upper lip. How did he not know about the hammer? Getting your news from the pub has its limitations—he should have been following the papers. There are four dead fathers now, every crime a duplicate of the first. That counts out the girls unless they knew each other and formed some kind of pact. That, or they were hypnotized? Not likely. The crimes could have been staged and the lasses drugged? He wanted to be sure though. He needed to speak with one. The girls aren't talking—in a trance, he heard. The one at the hospital, he would drag the truth out of her if he must.

Dooley watched the droves of suits outside quicken their stride to take cover from the thickening sheets of rain. So, it could be one man, or woman, he thought, just like he said to Cormac. Yet, what's in common between these killings, and the others? A hammer, disfigured faces, multiple killings spread over two or so weeks—he froze. Fourteen days? How's this Enoch writing this whole bloody book and posting it from Glasgow in fourteen days? The bloody maniac's in Dublin!

tv

"*Enoch,*

"*I'm sorry about your hand. I was caught up in the moment. I hope you know it was never my intention to cut it off; I was hoping for your head. But, I'd be upset if that happened too. Without you, I wouldn't be much right now, so I suppose I'm also prone to self-destruction. After that night a week ago, I feel more connected to you than ever. So, I ask you as a friend, how is your hand?*

"*I still cannot fathom why you came here; although I understand family obligations are hard to refuse. Myself, I've never lived in such a filthy and morally corrupt place. Even the hate is shallow. There's a reason though, a reason why the Indians are the way they are, and the whites as well. I'm not from this 'Little Crossing Over Place' as the Indians here call it, but I've picked up a story or two about what lies underneath the Puget Sound. Have you heard of Wahalchoo?*

"*Before Denny[xxviii], Maynard[xxix] and Yesler settled here and made their fortunes, it was just Indians. One day, a starved young man in search of a spirit guide was hunting sea fowl near the beach. He was busy retrieving stray arrows upon a sea cliff when an ancient longhouse appeared, submerged under the dark green waters of the bay. Herds of elk and schools of salmon surrounded and swarmed above the massive cedar structure—and like a pearl of light emanating from inside the longhouse, Wahalchoo saw power and prosperity posited within it. He ran home to tell his father of the spirit power he found beneath the water instead of diving in to grab it. When he returned, the longhouse was gone, and with it his opportunity.*

"*Nearly twenty years later settlement started here and it didn't take long*

40

for the Indians to recognize despite the apparent social harmony shared between them and the Dennys and Maynards and Borens and Yeslers, the longhouse under the sea was not going to reappear for Wahalchoo or any other Indian. Control over their own destiny settled somewhere at the bottom of the Puget Sound and the best they could do was incorporate into the fold, or at least to maintain a semblance of good humor in the face of change.

"Their story is not divorced from a Highlander's, no? I can just imagine a Highlander looking over a sea cliff watching ol' Bonnie Prince Charlie's gunship sink to the bottom of the ocean.[xxx] But, these events are inevitable; progress is always so cruel.

"Wahalchoo grew up to live in a shack at the edge of town until he was forced to move onto a reservation. I was told he died there not too long ago under the Christian name of Jacob and was survived by a Jack-Russell Terrier.[xxxi]

His collection of tin cups and other random objects were divided amongst his neighbors, and his story of the longhouse is still told but as a joke. See Enoch, so things do work out—not all stories end in tragedy.[xxxii]

"Now, I tell you this not because I care, but because you need to know this story did not escape the ears of the City Council.[xxxiii] They're all seeking the longhouse. Many of the Indians call Yesler's mill the longhouse, especially those he's employed throughout the past three decades. Even from the beginning, Denny and Maynard's obsession with proving Seattle's economic legitimacy and dominance in the region was for the sake of finding the longhouse's spirit power. And, of course, J. Colman—your benefactor: "the Scotsman who brought the railroad to Seattle"—he too is in search of Wahalchoo's claim. Burke, Gillman, Furth: These men are savages and they have the idiot masses of ignorant immigrants, backward pioneers, drunks and whores praising their every empty word.

"Let them all burn. History will strangle the archaic traditions of the Indians. As for Yesler and the like, I cannot stomach the thought they find the longhouse; it's not their right. It should forever remain lost. There's a right and wrong way to progress and if it can't be done right, perhaps it can be stopped from happening at all. Akin to how war freezes time.

"You can feel the lawlessness here, can you not? Blame Yesler for his lottery and the ugly crooks it attracted. Blame the City Council's vice licenses,

which fill the city's coffers more so than any other enterprise. This is where you were sent: to a city that makes its wealth from drink, sex and gambling.*xxxiv*

"We're different, neither native nor settler, we're outsiders. I admit, I'm losing myself to the subjective hammer. Even so, there's a cure, as I've come to know there's no such thing as a bystander here. You cannot be passive in the face of impending doom. Yet, after I cut off your hand and let you live, I realized killing to kill is not enough. So, I plan to be more creative about who dies to keep progress at bay. Know my movements have meaning.

"I have one last thing to add, you angered me in the stables. Your self-pity makes you ignorant to the death of worlds. You're a beast of progress because you refuse to acknowledge your complicity. You're indeed an advocate of reduction until you refuse to be and take action. Oh, but alas your self-loathing! Your narcissism needed to end, and if losing your hand was the universe's way to tell you to let go, so be it. As the saying goes, when one glove has been dropped, throw its match out the train window. People have it worse than you, Enoch. I watched my mother kill my father and then herself. I care little for fathers who mistreat their children—No little girl should have to live after what he did to her. She was the lone glove, I the arm, and my hammer, the window.

"Enoch, upon your recovery I encourage you to think deeper when you return to McGilvra's firm. There are sinister plots at work there. Perhaps Wahalchoo's longhouse is right under your nose. These men are devil worshipers of the worst kind. Their defining movements occur within the shadows. They shall burn soon."

"I'm sure this is the first time you've felt lucky to be left-handed?"

"To be sure, sir," I said, feeling less than so.

He showed me into the unused and dark filing room at the back of the law office.

"How're you finding things here with McGilvra's people?"

"It's paralegal work…" I stopped to change my tone as not to sound ungrateful, —which is a perfect opportunity for me to become acquainted with the likenesses and differences of our system to the Americans'."

"Your initial thoughts between their law and our Scots?"

"hypocritical, sir," I said.

"How?"

"Their law appears to be as careful and as well designed as ours, but in practice, I see no law."

James Colman—my benefactor—inspected my face. xxxv

"How do you mean?"

"Law controls man's impulse and greed, and protects our property and our health. Personal justice holds no weight in Scotland anymore. There are no duels, no revenge killings, and no misuse of power which goes unpunished. What of Yesler's scantlings? The mob? Seattle's vice licenses? The Indian reservations?"

"Don't be so blind to think these things no longer take place in Scotland. That the lineage of law and order is longer in Scotland means man has found more inventive ways to corrupt it. Take for example, the mills and tenements, are they not full of Highland descendants? Are they not the result of the Highland clearances? Can we not call them their own reservations?"

Colman appeared agitated.

"I'm sorry lad, but know this, all men are together guilty for the sins against humanity."

"But, what of the killings here?" I said. "Are they not heinous?"

"And no worse than those of London?" he responded. [xxxvi] "I more than regret promising not to write to your father concerning the killings. I should be sending you straight home."

"You know what the truth would do to my father and mother."

"Aye, we've been over that. Poor thing, your mother."

"It is," I said, but not stated as such to play up his pity. Colman met my mother only once, the year I was born. After which, the handful of times I remember meeting him was over tea in the city. His features haven't changed.

Mr. Colman was sturdy. Of medium build and height. His sharp face and tight eyes added deep shadows to his rock-hard face. He was always serious, like a devout Calvinist, but he was not as religious as much as he was business. Colman celebrated million dollar ideas, and solidifying his interests within Seattle at that altar. A man already thinking of his legacy before his legitimacy, in Seattle he became an out-of-towner too big to ignore.

"I told your father I would keep you out of trouble, and now I hear this madman has taken a liking to you. That, and now he's taken your hand—Ah well, what are we to do with you?"

"We do nothing. I'll learn to do everything with one hand."

"And, about this madman? —The whole town is in a panic."

Colman turned and drew the shades of the dark office's sole window to find a full frame of the adjacent building's wood siding no more than an arm's length distance. He appeared not to mind and cocked his head, inspecting the rippled skin of the untreated and weathered siding. "Nothing but rotten wood," he muttered.

"I'm sorry, sir?" I said, alluding out of formality to have not heard him.

"I've told you to call me James—This demon, Enoch," he continued, regaining his focus, "when this mess started people wouldn't leave their homes—and now how safe is one's own home after this? Some are blaming the bloody Indians. You don't think the killer is an Indian, do you?"

"I don't believe so, sir," I said, not wanting to add anything to stoke the conversation. I didn't want to talk about the killer; the image of the dead girl from the alleyway still bled in my mind.

"To think he killed a whole family—even the children. I knew John Edmonds well—a good man—did well without a wife." Colman turned to face me. "A huge supporter of the railroad. He helped coordinate the town picnic and was one on the first shovels in the ground when we laid down the rails.[xxxvii] A tragedy it is."

I looked at the section of plank flooring beside my right foot which my missing hand would've normally obstructed. My missing appendage reappeared, translucent and weightless. Colman coughed to regain my attention.

"Yes James, disgusting," I said.

I was still distracted. In my imagination, while Colman spoke, the room became the alleyway, the crime scene from last week. The dead girl peeled her body from its muddy floor. She proceeded to float away after spitting on her father's remains and glided past Butterfield and the onlookers. She turned around the corner and was gone. I wanted to follow.

Colman interjected again, snapping me away from the alley.

"No disrespect lad, but you seem distracted and look half dead. Go back to Lou Graham's and get some more rest. I'll make sure you have a girl set aside to see to your recovery."

I didn't know how to answer. One more day of lying down with my own memories, the sensation of pins and needles pricking away at a hand which no longer existed, along with the fear of another letter from my attacker made Lou's 'hotel' the last place I wanted to be. I was happy to stay inside McGilvra's firm and work—I would have typed a deposition with my nose rather than spend another second in bed.

"Solace and recovery is in hard work, sir," I parroted. "That's what my father said before my move to America, and now I fear it rings true. My place is here and I plan to help in any capacity I can."

Colman raised his eyebrows and his eyes lit up.

"Good man! Your father's boy you are." He put his hand on my shoulder. "You've had a rough time of it boy, but things will come right. Better you stay here than return home—no better place to become a better man."

I swallowed what contempt his statement triggered inside me and nodded.

"Well, I must be off, business from out of town is to arrive; matters of land and development to discuss. Not to mention this bloody dock I have been pushing for."

"Thinking ahead, sir?" I asked—the murderer's tale of the longhouse coming to mind.

"Our rails made it to the coal mines, but quarries only hold so much; they need to stretch farther. We Scots know about that business. Yes, there's plenty of opportunity in Seattle. Where a population grows, there's the need for expansion. I reckon responding to that need will keep me busy and the people happy."

"Aye sir, that is so, that is so."

Colman took a good look at me and smoothed his balding head with the plain of his large white hand. He plucked a watch from his waistcoat pocket, checked it, and grimaced. He snapped it shut and glanced at my missing hand.

"Let Mrs. Colman at least cook you supper."

"No, James I couldn't have—"

"You have little choice in the matter, it's either that or I'll have you gagged and sent back to Glasgow, despite my promise."

"You leave me little choice. I thank you and Agnes for your generosity."

"It'll be brought to your room this evening."

Colman walked out of the room and I stood alone inspecting the rotten wooden planks from out the window. I wondered where the little girl from the alley floated off to and what plans the killer entertained for Colman. But, perhaps the killer wasn't ready yet? I felt he was new at his trade, frightened he took things too far and couldn't stop what he'd started. Afraid of important people and daylight; of himself, and the faces he'd destroyed and collected inside his memory.

Vi

When I finished with my work, I stepped out of my makeshift office to find McGilvra's lawyers all gone. I was alone except for Charles, McGilvra's assistant. He was thin and tall and carried a slight limp he said he acquired from a childhood accident. His features were ordinary besides his bottom lip which was split down the middle and appeared as though it were a permanent feature to his face. We spoke very little, which was in line with many other locals I have met. Upon our first introduction, he struggled to understand my accent and ever since avoided me in a cold sort of way, displaying a nervous timidity, which is common among many here in Seattle. However, on this occasion, Charles appeared keener to engage with me than usual.

"Good afternoon, Charles," I said. "Will you be working late, or making your way home soon?"

"I, I beg your pardon, Mr. Enoch?"

"Just Enoch."

"Yes, Enoch."

"I asked if you'll be on your way home soon?"

"Mr. McGilvra wired from San Francisco—There are stacks on stacks of documents belonging to Mr. Colman I need to order and file, along with a flurry of easements and such I have to investigate on behalf of Mr. Jacob Furth and his water works." He paused and then continued. "Do you mind reading over a short letter I wrote on Mr. Furth's behalf for any errors or incongruences?"

Charles appeared anxious, but he always was.

"Mr. Furth's water works?"

"Yes, could you? I'll owe you one," he said.

"Aye, hand it here."

I returned to my desk.

"To the Mayor,

"It is obvious at this point our water pressure and the reach of our water system is no longer sufficient to service our growing population. As well, the archaic composition of our pipes serves as a ticking time bomb, which has already erupted in certain areas of the city. A massive overhaul of our young city's water and sewer systems is a high priority if Seattle wishes to be called a "modern city."

"To date, there have been many complaints to do with sinkholes, lack of water pressure, and lack of water siphoning up to the higher sections of the city. This will simply not do. I, in congress with city and private engineers and John McGilvra's legal team, are working together to produce a full report as to the physical reasons behind the failure of our current water system, the ways to fix the issue, and the best method toward enacting these updates. However, I must be transparent here and say as of now, there is no answer as to how we are to replace an intricate system of rotting pipes buried beneath our city's current structures. It could take years, if not a decade or two, to see this conversion completed.

"However, Seattle is a city full of pragmatic optimists and blessed with a business core who are relentless in their drive to see the city prosper for the benefit of all. Indeed, there is an answer to this situation, and we will find it.

Your humble servant,

Jacob Furth
Spring Hill Water Company[xxxviii]"

I looked up from the letter and indeed found it troublesome. To know the extent of the city's decay also existed beneath the soil, to its very foundation, filled me with dread. I suppose, I was worried about my father's investments in the city, but also, worried about myself. Was this related with the killer's warnings?

I turned to my handless side, and the faceless girl stood next to me, holding my severed hand as a child would their father's. She then vanished and my hand dropped to the floor with a thud. It rapidly decomposed until just bones. I stood up and left the room.

"Here it is," I said, stamping it down on a stack of files perched on Charles's desk.

"Is anything the matter?" he said.

"My hand hurts."

"But you have no hand."

He eyed me as if I were mad.

"Sometimes it feels like it's still there," I said.

"I used to feel this way about my brother," he said, lifting and placing the letter he showed me in front of him.

"I'm sorry for your loss," I said.

"Thank you, but it was years ago. Did you find any issues with the correspondence?"

"If there are, they're of a different nature—the letter is fine."

"Good," he said. "Let us hope they find a way to improve the city."

"Yes, let us pray they find a way."

Vii

In the high tower of our castle off Byres Road I would escape from my unhappy parents. Perched inside Bessy's face I'd look out upon Glasgow and think of Spain, or any place for that matter, with sun and people with tanned skin. The city could be so lonely, and the constant grey, maddening. Inside Bessy, it was the same—solemn.

I was reading my favorite book, *Kidnapped,*[xxxix] when a wail crept up the tower. I looked up,—coincidentally, I was reading the chapter where at the House of Shaws, the young David Balfour was forced by his uncle, Ebenezer to climb the dark tower of the old crumbling house without a candle—and closed the book, afraid I was being beckoned into my own trap. The wail came again and louder than the last. It was my mother.

I descended the narrow staircase and crept toward her room. I put my ear to the door and listened. I heard nothing for a minute, but then a rustle which sounded very close. I turned to check behind me, but no one was there. While my head was still turned the door opened, and my mother grabbed my shirt and tugged me inside. I fell to the floor and watched the light escape the room as she slammed the door shut. The shutters were closed and the curtains drawn leaving the room pitch black. All was still but the sound of my mother's feet shuffling across the room away from me.

"Mother," I said, but there was no answer. "Mother," I repeated.

She struck a match and the burn-up of the sulfur coordinated with the twisted look on her face as she watched the flame grow onto the matchstick. She peered at me and then to the oil lamp on the bureau beside her.

"Are you my living son or the dead one?" She said, lighting the lamp.

"I'm your only son."

"No!" she said. "There are duplicates of everything, and I need to know now, which Enoch are you?"

"I'm the dead one."

"I thought so," she said, smiling. "I love you, Enoch."

One of me loved her too.

·   ·   ·   ·   ·

The clouds tumbled in from the southwest, and over the Olympic peaks.[xl] The Brothers[xli] presented ominous and up to something sinister. I could see a wall of grey push inland over the back of Elliott Bay and squeeze between a broken string of shabby looking buildings on 2nd Avenue. Smoke and dust from Yesler's Wharf mixed with it and the drizzle. I turned to a small white church sitting lonely on the corner and thought how out of place it was.[xlii] The little faceless girl walked out of the church, through the graveyard, and ran past me. I wanted to give chase, but I was weak. My right arm throbbed and felt infected.

Despite this, the cool air felt good and soon refreshed me. I wanted to stay outside and investigate the city—maybe I'd stumble upon a clue to help me figure out what the killer would do next. I interpreted my hallucination of the girl as a sign, even though her ghost was brutal to look at. This must be how my mother interpreted the ghosts she saw. Her eyes would always wander, and I knew it was because she was seeing things. I figured, perhaps if I followed the girl I'd learn something about the killer, and possibly, something about my mother.

The streets were busy. Wagons and the occasional streetcar clapped through, and in between men conversing on tilted and slick fir-plank boardwalks. Some men gathered on the street level, and others congregated atop the shabby wooden staircases which led to the doors of businesses elevated above the ground to clear the street's steep grade. Submerged on these steep hills, Seattle's wooden structures, and even the newer stone ones, floated like sinking ships with one end higher than its opposite. Nothing was level in Seattle. Every street rippled like an undulating wave. I passed the alley where the body of the girl and her father once laid. In the daylight, void of onlookers and policemen, it stood unsatisfied and common. There she was. Standing on the corner. Faceless. She floated north and then vanished. The pain in my arm seized and the blood in my head mixed with whatever dangerous chemistry I inherited from my mother. I fought the pain and doubled my pace.

I passed inkblots of businessmen in fur hats and patterns of women hidden in layers of embroidered dresses. As I marched on they became fewer, and instead, the lower classes, the natives and half-castes, and the Chinese who hover near the Lava Beds, reappeared. The mixing of peoples in Seattle is a constant—and the peripheral areas of town are not the only places where the unwanted dwell. However, gaining north, their presence was short lived. In a matter of a block the density of the city center diminished. The street's increased incline was to blame. My legs began to burn.

I could feel my temperature rise as I climbed up 2nd. I passed Marion, Madison and Spring Streets—sweat leaking out onto my brow from under my hat. I cut down Seneca Street, passing the skating rink, and onto Front Street. The girl appeared again and pointed down the street towards Madison and then burst into flames. I stood still not knowing where to go until I saw her burnt body a block north holding the hand of a blurry figure. The figure was a twisted storm of flies, an amorphous smudge, akin to a greasy fingerprint on a glass negative.

There were even fewer people around and the girl appeared again, no longer burnt, but back in her dress and alone. I tried to gain on her, but I couldn't and she refused to turn around to look at me. The streets were very steep now and full of some of the largest homes I'd yet seen in Seattle. The girl turned down Union Street onto West Avenue. She hit Pike and turned left again and the Puget Sound was in full view as was a small enclave of dismal wooden huts amongst a few skinny pines and miles of ruddy coastline. The contrast was sharp. The wooden cabins were built piecemeal with random planks scaled to create walls, and weathered cedar shingles covered the roofs in a haphazard pattern broken up with a missing shingle, or a fresh shingle still glowing bright red.

I walked closer to the huts and was surrounded by the scattered features of tin buckets, shovels and discarded seashells. On the slanted porch of one I saw a very old Indian woman sitting at the foot of her door obscured in layers of clothing, a blanket over her shoulders, and a scarf around her head. She sat quite still and it was hard to tell if she was awake or asleep. I was about to turn and leave, feeling out of place and indeed uncomfortable with fever, when she waved to me. I waved back and greeted her with my name, but her response was too quiet for me to hear, so I walked closer.

Clothing was set on a sloped fence which guarded half the entrance to her home. Beside her small stool was a pile of half-woven baskets. I stood at the foot of the steps and waited. I didn't know what to say, and I was also not aware if she could understand me; I didn't have much experience with Indians.

"I'm Angeline," she said, "Princess Angeline. I wash clothes. Do you need washing?"

I considered what I was wearing and then looked back at her and said no. We sat in silence as the darkness surged closer from the Olympics.

"You look sick," she said, "there are white doctors in town."

"My hand was cut off a week ago."

"I was told about this. You chased the killer."

"Yes."

She made a sound of interest, but said nothing.

"There's a storm. Come back when you have clothes needing washing."

She rose from her chair, turned the small brass knob of her door, and slipped into the black crease inside her home. The door closed and I thought I was alone until I turned around and about thirty yards away a middle-aged Indian man stood at the foot of his door staring at me.

"You should go home, there's a storm," he yelled with his hands cupped around his mouth.

I nodded, tipped my hat, and gave one last glance out onto the water. I saw the little girl in her white dress walking on the water towards the darkness. The busy smudge of flies beside her.[xliii]

·   ·   ·   ·   ·

An aura of orange light engulfed my mother's slight body. She stepped towards me and grew darker, but the features of her face shined through the dim light. Her madness pulled at her skin, but she still looked like the woman I remembered from my childhood. Her eyes were small, nose sharp, and lips made of glass. Her neck was a column of strain which over time ate away at her breasts beneath her nightgown. I wondered, was she my living or dead mother?

"Your father is planning to send me away," she said.

"No mother, that's not true."

"But it is."

"May I open the shutters to bring in some light?" I said.

"No."

"Why not?"

"I can see them if there's too much light."

"Who?" I said.

"I don't know, but they're faceless."

"Mother."

We sat in the dark, the glow of the lantern lessening from lack of fuel.

"I love you, mother," I said to make her feel comfortable.

The room was silent and I listened to the dying lantern suck for oxygen.

"You father will send you away one day, and you'll need to make a choice."

I didn't understand or know how to respond.

"I'm so sorry, but someday you're going to have to die," she said, growing agitated.

"It's okay, mother; we all die," I said.

"Let the right one die—you have to promise me."

"I promise."

I could see through the receding light that she was still distressed.

"I'll make the right choices," I said. "I'll make sure to save the right one."

She began to cry, and I pawed for her shoulders. She shuttered when I found her.

"It's me," I said.

I held her and she nuzzled my neck. I felt like crying too.

"I'm so sorry," she said.

The lantern went out, and she screamed like she'd been stabbed in the back. I let go of her and retreated for the door. I was lost in the room and my mother was still screaming. The door swung open and white light poured into the dark room. I turned and saw the ghost that was my mother. Her eyes bulged, red around their edges, and her exposed shoulders resembled goat hooves sharpened into blades.

"Shut the door!" she said. "You're letting in the flies and she needs to rest."

"Come on, Enoch," My father said. "You're not meant to be in here."

I walked out of the room and looked back at my mother; she appeared as though she was holding someone's hand.

Viii

I was already exhausted and still needed to hike up the bluffs to Front Street. The rain rolled in and pitter-pattered upon the shoulders of my heavy coat in a rhythm of dull flicks. My body felt like it was on fire. With only one hand to hold my coat, I was afraid if I were to carry it, the weight would tip me over. I needed something. I needed Lou to save me.

I made it onto Front Street. The plainness of the district and the formulaic construction of the large houses stood in stark contrast to the encampment below them. The contrast reminded me of my home in Glasgow versus the factories not a mile away from it. The deep creases of Princess Angeline's face burned in my mind.

Lou said the settlers have fought hard for years to push the Indians out of the city. But, despite the reservation across the water, and the encampments on the peripheries of town, Indians are woven into the fray of daily life. The Indians wear pants and jackets, and dress just like the whites. The men work in the mills and on the docks and the women do the washing and keep tidy the houses of the rich. Many more come into the city to trade. Some wander the streets near Skid Road and the Lava Beds, but not the majority.

Full bloods and half-castes commingle with the whites and the Chinese and the Hawaiians. Indians from far north come here to work. Lou looks for mixed Indian girls to hire because the men enjoy them. And though it's illegal, white men marry Indian girls.

Indian canoes are still pulled ashore onto Elliott Bay. They lay next to cedar smoke racks stuffed with belts of salmon eggs and fat fillets of red-fleshed salmon. A rich fishy bouquet permeates the waterside taverns and brothels. The settlers, even those who have moved here from San Francisco for business, and many of the Chinese, can speak in Indian jargon.[xliv] The tongue is strange, as strange as Erse was to Lowlanders a long time ago, and still to us Scotsmen who visit the isles off the coast. But, how long can this mixing continue being it's considered one of the city's failures? The smell of smoked fish bears likeness to the dust of old books.

In his letter, the killer made sense; perhaps he knows what's going to happen, the inevitable decay of the past, or at least the slow absorption of its practitioners. The future hates what already was. That hate is prevalent here. The men who want Seattle to grow for profit, rule. A direct rail line to the East and California would do it. Seattle would be bigger than Tacoma, and would win the imagination of those in America who want a so-called better life.

It's natural—though repugnant—to want more and more. Until I lost my hand I never cared about wealth one way or another, but now I can hold onto half what I used to, and so fear for want. I long for all the things I can't carry—the dead things, too. It's a paradox I want to die sometimes, but want my hand back to carry things. I want the dead girl's ghost to reappear, or for me to be light enough to walk out onto the water with her and search for Wahalchoo's claim. To be consumed by the storm of flies and be fine with it.

•   •   •   •   •

I vomited on the side of the road. I worried about being noticed, but the rain thickened into a sopping screen, and everyone besides a few children playing in the puddles up the street withdrew from the sidewalks for shelter. Nonetheless, I did what I could to hide my performance, and when I felt better pulled a kerchief from my pocket to wipe my mouth. I felt embarrassed but refreshed and cooler. The rain will wash it away.

I continued down Front Street and Madison. A block ahead, along the side of the opulent, if not out of place opera house stood a group of boys in a circle looking down at something. The wee ones in the back were frantically beating their bodies in between the legs of their older brothers to catch a glimpse of whatever was happening. I closed in and noticed the boys were standing around a large hole. It rippled from the falling rain. The stucco walls of the opera house were glistening wet.

An older boy ran out of a chemist[xlv] located on the ground level of the French-looking theater. The business's elderly owner was right behind the boy with a long-handled broom in his hand. More adults fled from their dry shelters and the opera house's large awnings to the hole and began to pluck the children from its crumbling edge until only the chemist remained, kneeling on the ground with his arm submerged in the pool of water. He stirred the stick end of the broom around to feel for something, or for someone to grab a hold of it.

"It's Jacob!" a woman yelled back to a group of other women amassed underneath a dripping shop-front sill. "The boy was taken by a sinkhole!"

Once the news was broadcasted, the rain ceased to matter to anyone and they ran out onto the street to gain a look. A tavern owner sprang from his front door with a coil of heavy rope and pushed through the crowd while tying its end into a loop. The old chemist stood up from the muddy ground and wiped his soiled arms on his white apron—his broom was lost in the hole. Outside the theater, the crowd grew by the minute and appeared entertained by the spectacle. Some even laughed at the men around the hole when they stumbled over each other trying to save the child.

More men broke through the crowd to help. The butcher ran out with a cured whole pig's head and front quarters to tie on the end of the rope as a weight. One man slipped and fell into the hole, which caused the crowd to erupt in hysterics. He was pulled out and then the rope was lowered into the brown abyss, taking coil after coil with it until it was drawn back up. The men inspected the mud line at the last coil to the pig's ear. I measured from my vantage point the depth of the hole was three yards. There was a hurried discussion between them and they removed the pig's head from the rope. It sat macerated in mud, grinning at the crowd. The tavern owner put his foot through the loop at the rope's end and lowered himself into the hole while the other men held the slack and braced for leverage to lower him in. The man disappeared into the hole and with him the voices of the onlookers.

The father showed up beside himself. The crowd was a mob now and there began episodes of infighting between those in the crowd laughing it up and the others worried about the boy's doomed fate.

"Ahh Jesus, the boy's daddy is paying for it now," he said, "he's always letting him run round with no leash. He shudda known bout that hole, I wudda thought."

I looked back, and a middle-aged man with a black mustache and a clouded eye noticed and turned his face to give his good eye a chance to scan my face.

"Where's his house?" I asked.

"I don't reckon I know you, sir."

"Beg your pardon, my name is Enoch Campbell. I work at J.J. McGilvra's law firm."

"You then are the foreigner consorting with the devil in town," he growled, and causing those bystanders close to us to turn, "I wish the lot of you foreigners would go back to New York where you landed."

"Excuse me…" I began, before I was interrupted by a strong voice located beside me.

"Gentlemen, if you please. There's a boy drowning in your midst, I doubt this is the most opportune time to get into a disagreement," Lou said. She squeezed the back of my arm to intimate she was speaking upon my behalf. "Though, Mr. Richards," she added, "you seem to find little wrong with my establishment being founded by a German, nor do you seem unhappy with my foreign girls' knowledge of opera."

The milk-eyed Mr. Richards worked hard to count the quick glances the preoccupied crowd gave him before they returned their attention to the sinkhole and the tavern owner's second attempt to save the boy.

Lou pushed me away to the periphery of the crowd and took a long hard look at me.

"What are you doing here?" she asked, sounding upset with me.

"Opera?"

"Don't even dare, Enoch. Every man, no matter how they appear, has his surprises."

"I wasn't, Lou. He just seemed too great a bastard…"

"To enjoy opera? Tell me who's not a bastard that listens to opera?"

"Steady on, Lou."

"Steady, what?" she said.

"Nothing."

"Now not another word, Enoch. You look like you're near death. You need to get back to bed."

"I'm not well," I said.

There was a loud gasp from the audience and jeers spit from the back as the tavern owner surfaced empty handed. The crowd reveled in the disappointment and grew more agitated. Astonished faces swiveled around to find those exhibiting joy, but the chaotic smiles from those who can't help but show excitement in the face of tragedy paid the empathetic little attention. The crowd was a mob now, and many asked around if there was a better swimmer than the tired barkeep. Shouts sprang out for a doctor, and when one appeared the crowd parted and cheered his entrance. It was Dr. Tom from the alley murder. His little frame seemed to inflate with the crowd's cheers. I couldn't look at him without becoming dizzy. His skin was green.

It was either Lou reminding me of my deteriorated condition or the bizarre behavior of the mob, but whichever was responsible, I began to feel as though my soul was lifting away from my head. I stumbled and Lou caught me and stood me up.

"We need to get you out of here."

"But the boy?" I said.

She pushed me further away, onto the boardwalk, and helped me down a short flight of steps when another cheer erupted from the crowd. Up from the hole came the barkeep. The boy's father snatched his son from the man's arms and shook the limp body for a sign of life. The barkeep collapsed to the ground, exhausted. The crowd cheered. The boy was brown as a chocolate. The pig grinned, victorious.

"Like Pompeii," I gasped.

Lou gave herself the sign of the cross.

"The poor boy," she whimpered, "the poor boy."

"His poor mother," I said.

Lou shot me a confused look.

The crowd began to push and swirl while the onlookers at the back began to push for a peek at the dead boy.

"There will no doubt be a petition to fix our streets come tomorrow," Lou said.

"You can't fix what just happened."

She peered at me—through me—and said:

"You can always start over, Enoch; isn't that why you're here?"

"I'm here by my father's will."

"It's more than that, and you know it."

I refused one girl already when a second knocked on my door.

"Thank you," I said, "but I wish to be alone."

"Madame Lou sent me to cool your fever," the London accent responded through the door.

"Tell her thank you, but I wish to be alone."

"I can't."

"What do you mean you can't?"

"Lou said she would no longer require my services if you didn't let me in."

Damn Lou.

"You can come in, but I don't want anything."

The door opened and the girl I'd seen the night I lost my hand, entered. Her face was dusted with powder and her body was bound up in a corseted yellow dress. She was holding a small porcelain dish with a cloth folded and draped over her forearm. Her hair was done up in an ornate bun and black ringlets fell to the side of her narrow face.

"Where would you like me, sir?"

"Enoch."

She didn't answer. The seat next to the fireplace was filled with my wet clothes and I attempted to get up to remove them. I failed. She set down the bowl on the fireplace mantle and removed the clothes herself.

"These will need to be washed," she said, "I'll send them down."

I was amid a dizzy spell and clung to my mattress.

"Sir?" she said in a worried tone, attempting to help me.

"No," I said.

She stopped herself in mid stride and looked foolish paused in her advance and I felt as though I hurt her with my abruptness.

"It's Enoch. If the chair isn't too wet you can sit there. The clothes can go on the floor."

She stood still for a second to regain her composure and then set the clothes down before sitting on the chair.

"I'm sorry, it's just that—"

"I know," she said, ironing her dress pleats with her hands.

I didn't know what to say so I concentrated instead on staving off the images of the faceless little girl and the drowned boy.

"What's your name?" I asked.

"Anna."

"Anna what?"

"Anna Cameron."

"I'm sorry I was rude."

The room remained cold and silent. She looked away from me and to the rain splattered window panes letting in the muted light of the grey afternoon.

"You're English," I said. "What on earth are you doing here?"

"I came from New York."

"But, why Seattle?"

"I was told there's more opportunity here. I signed some papers to join a sowers' guild." She became sullen, and played with the embroidery of her dress. "Not what I was expecting," she said.

"I didn't have a choice either," I said. "I was forced away to tend to my father's business."

"Yes, but clearly not the same thing?"

Clearly it wasn't.

"Fair enough," I said. "I'm sorry."

I felt awkward and uncreative with my words. I was shit with women and her personal story made me uncomfortable. I didn't care about what she did for a living, but that she was forced into it made it near impossible for me not to feel bad.

"It's your father's business to send his son into the woods, is it?" she said.

"I suppose so," I said. "Lou's told you about me?"

"She's told me enough. With the killings, you're the talk of the house."

"Why?"

"The killer writes to you, does he not?"

"Yes."

"And you chased him to the livery where you lost your hand?"

A ghost spasm ran through my invisible appendage.

"I did, and it was stupid."

"A death wish," she said.

She stood up, took a match from the fireplace and lit a cigarette. She took a long drag and then propped her elbow on the mantle. Her disposition changed, like she was pretending before to be timid.

"I don't know what I was thinking," I said.

"Well, the girls here are afraid. Some of them are curious about you, but most of us want you out."

Why?" I said.

"Because the killer is bound to show up here at some point," she said. "Girls in our line of work are already terrified and the last thing we need is an out-of-towner attracting some lunatic to bash our faces in."

"I'll be gone soon."

Anna took another drag of her cigarette.

"Listen, you should do yourself a favor and get out of Seattle."

"The killer isn't going to kill me," I said.

"Don't be so sure," she said.

I was surprised by her lack of confidence in my mortality.

"Aye?"

"Aye, you bloody Scot, stop being so proud and know when you're cornered."

She began to tremble and appeared frightened. I didn't believed her anger was directed towards me; it was directed somewhere else.

"Who's cornering me?" I said.

"You don't know, and no one who does will say, that's the problem," she said.

She walked to my bedside and leaned in.

"Girls have disappeared, long before the killer arrived."

"What're you getting at?"

She ashed her cigarette in the bowl she'd entered with.

"Look," she said, refusing to look in my direction, "we hear things. All the drink that runs through here and the businessmen, you hear a lot. Sometimes, we hear too much." She looked at me square. "I've heard things I shouldn't have and sometimes that means we go away."

"What kind of things?" I asked.

"About the future," she said.

She walked over and collected my clothes and then stood at the door.

"Between you and me, hide your letters."

She opened the door and stepped out without saying another word.

I laid in my bed, scared. It was the first time since arriving I felt completely unwanted. I thought of the Indian woman, Angeline, and regretted not keeping my laundry for her. It was a strange thought. Anna seemed to know something, but so did the woman. I hated being in the dark. The room was dark. I missed my mother. I even missed Glasgow.

I woke from my nap and felt better but lonely as though the world died in my absence. The rain outside smacked against the window with every gust of wind. The bass notes from the piano downstairs crawled up the legs of my bed frame and the pulse of conversation buzzed the floorboards underneath. The world still turned. I lit the oil lamp beside my bed. I thought maybe Anna was right, I was endangering her and the rest of Lou's girls.

I felt an undeniable urge to drink whisky. I dressed and crept downstairs. My hope was to cross the main drawing room and saloon without attracting Lou's attention. However, since the door was at the far end of the main congregation, my chances of avoiding detection were slim. I made my way through the clouds of consorting gentlemen and women and was nearly to the door when a strong hand grasped my shoulder. I turned and it was the gentleman with the clouded eye I'd met earlier on the street.

"Spectin a n'other murder tonight, young man?" he said.

"No sir, just a hangover come tomorrow morning."

"Hard fer you Scots ta understand but public displays of drunkenness aren't kind topics of dis'cussion for us folk."

"Unintended, Mr. Richards."

He gave another patronizing smile and nodded.

I began to turn away to escape when he grabbed my right arm and clutched it tight, causing a dull belt of lightning to shoot out from my stumped wrist.

"My god, man!" I said, just under the volume of the piano.

"I know it's you," he whispered in my ear.

A smallish man with greying wiry hair and a full goatee appeared beside us holding a glass of bourbon in one hand and a napkin held underneath its bottom by the other. He smiled. His blue suit was at odds with the other men in black mingling in Lou's drawing room.

"I hope we're not quarreling over the same woman?"

His slight Czech accent soothed the tone of his interruption.

"Mr. Furth[xlvi]," Richards greeted.

"Mr. Richards, I see you've introduced yourself to our town's newest arrival."

Furth put his hand on my back looking at Richards until my accuser released his grip.

"Yes, I dare say we have," Richards said.

"This's good. And beg your pardon, but if you may excuse us, I have yet to become acquainted with the young advocate from Glasgow, and I have some business to discuss with him at the request of Mr. McGilvra."

"We were finished anyway, Mr. Furth," I said.

I turned my back on them both and took a step closer to the door.

"Enoch."

I looked back and Richards dissolved into the mess of men. Furth stood sturdy with his left hand extended. We shook even though I felt anxious to part from his company. I couldn't detect anything about his presence to warrant being rude and so I relaxed as much as I could.

"I've heard your name mentioned at McGilvra's firm."

"I don't doubt it," Furth said. "McGilvra's lawyers handle many of the legal matters tied to the city projects I'm involved in."

"Like Charles."

"Yes, he's new, but very thorough."

I continued our exchange, careful not to reveal my knowledge of his prospective waterworks plan, or any other venture for that matter.

"My name's Jacob. Sorry to have interrupted your conversation with Mr. Richards, but I was told by Lou you were in need of saving."

"He's not fond of me," I said.

"Nor is he a fan of me. As a Czech Jew, I stand little chance of winning his affection."

"His favor is nothing I wish to win."

Furth shook his head.

"In business, you should be on everyone's best side no matter how glum the outlook."

"I reckon you have a point."

His smile sent his cheekbones high upon his heart-shaped face.

"Now, if I'm not mistaken you were present at the drowning?"

"Aye."

"I am ashamed of it."

"Why?"

The piano stopped playing at the beginning of my question and it hung in the air for a moment while Furth took in a deep breath to gather his thoughts. He sipped his drink and let it sit in his mouth.

"Would you care for a bourbon?" he said, after swallowing.

We walked over to the bar and faced each other with our ribs against its edge. My bourbon was delivered and I waited for Furth to begin.

"This town is crumbling just when it's becoming a true city," he said. "The death of this innocent young boy is disastrous and it draws attention to Seattle's rotten facilities."

"You mean, the sorry state of your streets?—Wooden pipes underneath I've been told."

"That's correct—the sewer pipes are rotting beneath us. The system could take years to replace and a lot of money."

"Luckily, you're a banker."

He took another drink.

"A banker is not as rich as his bank's net holdings."

"Aye, but you have credit and power, no?"

"And what kind of power do you believe I possess?"

"In Scotland, it's known bankers hold the loans."

"Yes, I can grant loans—If it's advantageous for the bank to do so."

"And access?"

"My business interests do put me in contact with others interested in Seattle's prosperity."

"I beg your pardon, but that sounds a wee overly altruistic. We're talking about businessmen are we not?"

He laughed.

"Yes, we are, but personal capital gain and public benefit are not mutually exclusive ventures; the investor and the citizen can both gain," he said, still smiling. I found his grin disingenuous.

"In my experience, personal financial gain comes first, and residual public benefit—if any—follows, but is never necessary."

His lips shut and I could see his pupils flare.

"What do you know of the world, young man?" he quipped.

"I know of Yesler's lottery."

Furth's smile returned.

"Ah, so an instance of greed tells you Seattle is a greedy city?"

"It tells me Seattle is no different than any other city."

"Seattle is young and in competition with cities like Tacoma to survive."

"So, it's about winning?"

Furth shook his head and took a sip from his glass.

"The economic fertility of Seattle depends upon beating out its competition. This sole factor aligns the economic interests of Seattle to its citizens—every citizen, from the entrepreneur to the logger."

"What do they get paid with if you succeed, a tour through your second house?"

Furth scoffed.

"Your compatriot, James Colman is testament to residual benefits. His fortune in logging, coal and the railroad has not only benefited him, but has helped save Seattle from falling behind Tacoma. Without his rails to Newcastle we would be too far behind to catch up. The poor would be poorer."

"But, his rails aren't enough," I said.

"That's why we need to link our rails with Chicago and New York; that's our most important goal. To lose the race will spell catastrophe for Seattle's economy."

"Are the Indian's benefitting? —It doesn't appear so."

Furth looked down and gave a slight chuckle before turning his head to the barkeep and pointed to his drink to intonate he wanted another.

"I appreciate you're a moralist. It's our job to help them when we can, while also reminding them they will have to adapt and meet us halfway for their own prosperity."

"Aye, but in Scotland, when the landlords cleared the Highlands for Cheviot sheep, and the folk flitted down to Glasgow, what happened then? Twelve-hour days in the mill and three families sharing a single-end. Where's the "meeting halfway" in that?"

Furth lowered his eyes.

"And do you see anything like the abhorrent conditions of old Glasgow here? I say you do not."

"I see people sleeping upon mud floors on Skid Road, weans running wild and getting sucked into the street, and this is not to mention a mad man killing innocents at will in a town without anyone the wiser of how to catch him."

Furth's shoulders relaxed. His sudden change in demeanor made me anxious like I stepped into a trap.

"And unless I'm mistaken, you're the fearless outsider who's come to make things right?"

I saw the hole I dug for myself and realized I said too much. Now, I'd have to oblige him and talk about the killer. I finished my bourbon and asked for another—Furth demure about putting a second on his tab.

"I'm no detective," I said.

"Then just fascinated by mutilated corpses?"

"It helps," I said.

I stared at him as he kept up his smile.

"Sometimes our Czech humor comes out too dry, I meant nothing by it, but you must say it's a bit curious, your relationship with the killer?"

I was about finished with his smile.

"I became a witness the day I came here three weeks ago. I found the first body. Chief Butterfield asked my advice about the second. The third, Lou got wind of, and sent me there to help—the girl in the alley."

"And you ran after the killer to catch him?"

"Something like that," I said.

"I don't understand. You intended to catch him or not?" he said.

"Turning him into the police was not on my mind at the time."

I twisted my torso to lean on the bar. I felt warm from the bourbon.

"You wanted to kill him?" Furth asked, dropping his smile.

"After a while I wanted to, yes."

"But this is for the law to decide."

"What law? I'm not convinced there's law here."

"The same you up hold as an advocate, as an American lawyer. Are you not one of McGilvra's lawyers?"

"I am."

"Then how can you think of taking the law into your own hands?"

Furth appeared to be bothered.

"It was in the heat of the moment, and I paid for my overzealousness with my hand," I said, holding up my bandaged stump.

"I can sympathize with your desire to subdue the killer. Although, from now on, I would watch yourself and your connection with him. Mr. Richards is just one of a few who find the timing of your arrival and the beginning of the murders suspicious."

"Do they?"

"They do, and whispers have begun to fall into the ears of Butterfield."

"Butterfield knows better than that," I said.

"Public pressure can make men in his position desperate."

Furth winked at me and nodded as if he'd meant more by what he said.

Through the entire conversation, he'd been playing cute. I couldn't figure out what he wanted from me. One moment he sounded sympathetic, but the next, desperate for information. If I didn't know better, he knew something I didn't, and it exhibited power over me.

"I'm a close friend of Lou's," he said, "I'll do my best to keep you safe. Now, she tells me the killer writes you letters?"

"Aye, he writes to me," I said. "He's developed his own kind of pseudo-philosophy. He thinks he can control history, like he can change its direction. "He bangs on about progress and cycles: what keeps recurring no matter the age."

"Cycles? History? Sounds like Hegel.[xlvii] Fascinating; the stadial model of progress? A tad dated though, isn't it?"

I gave Furth an inquisitive look; he was no fool.

"The study of Scots law is as deep into history as I go. A very linear way of going about history: 'what happened and how it changed things' type of view."

"The German school was not altogether divorced from the Scottish, but this is decades ago. Somewhat related, have you heard of Sigmund Freud?"[xlviii]

"No, but I take it he's German," I said.

"Austrian. His work to break down the human psyche is by all means divisive in the field of psychiatry. Haven't you always wondered if we have less control of our motives than we think? That there is a subconscious—as he says—conditioned by our past experiences informing and transforming our consciousness to act upon its bidding?"

"I haven't a clue what that means."

"That free will isn't as free as we think; we are prisoners inside our own histories. And like you said, keep making the same mistakes again and again until we have dealt with our past."

"And how do we know what experiences affect us or not?"

"He uses hypnosis to unlock his patients' secrets."

"He sounds like a quack."

I laughed, and he smiled with me.

"I dare say your assumption is a fair response for any man from the Isles to make."

My laughter subsided, but his smile remained.

"What's that supposed to mean?" I said.

"Can you not say the English and quite rightly, the Scots' own penchant for stoic reflection leads to a great deal of emotional repression?"

"You're explaining my father now, aren't you?"

"No, this is just for fun," he said, laughing.

"You sound like a Frenchman, Mr. Furth. We deal with what comes as it comes and deal with things as they happen. Misery and tragedy are the unhappy realities of living, but we must experience them and move on. We don't lament about them for years afterwards, or at least we confine our nostalgia to literature, where it can do ni harm."

"And confine your mother to her bedroom? I suppose every culture is different," Furth said, releasing his shoulders and softening his face to forestall the discussion becoming an argument. "Yet, control is the issue, and I wonder sometimes just how much control the killer has over his actions? Indeed, how much control do I have or you for that matter?"

We looked through a veil of intellectual smoke at each other and saw an impasse approach from the dark recesses of intuition. How did he know about my mother? Colman, I guessed.

"What's best for society is for its citizens to walk within the lines of the law," I said.

"But what if it starts breaking apart? Then what?"

I put my glass to my mouth and took the rest of the bourbon in.

"Then we fix it."

"Sometimes the whole edifice must be cleared for a better one to take its place," he said.

"Sounds like a slippery slope."

"Now, we've switched places," he said.

Dublin, 1916

The carriage jostled the intoxicated doctor from side to side as it clapped through the tilted brick streets of Dublin's Northside. The squawking of sea birds joined the hisses from a crowd of angry loiterers, offended by the presence of the doctor's carriage. Dooley peered out his carriage window and sneered back with equal disdain. "They could be the next murder victims and no one would care," he thought. "Take a hammer to the morally decrepit and leave our fathers in peace," he mumbled. He wanted more drink and was losing his urge to visit the sanitarium. His thoughts migrated to other matters of annoyance: Enoch's manuscript, his stupid little book. Dooley again cursed Enoch's proclivity for dramatics and digressive exposition and blamed he was drunk by noon on the young man's poor writing. He looked out the coach window and saw doubled buildings, blurry beggars and ghosts in the fog. He took a deep breath to keep from spinning. "What of this killer, or still, these hures?" he said. "In either case, what of these dead fathers so close to Easter?"

Yet, no matter how much he despised the manuscript, the doctor knew without it, he wouldn't have an adventure at all to keep him busy and his mind from his own problems. Enoch's troubled words drew him to the far reaches of the city to speak with a child murderer housed within St. Brendan's Richmond Asylum[xlix], and he would have to thank him for the privilege if he ever got the chance. Thomas Dooley imagined the horrid collection of pictures Enoch's descriptions placed there. The little girl in the dress whose face lay buried in the alley; the broken body of the father; the chocolate covered boar's head smiling beside the drowned boy; the red-skinned woman swathed in blankets.

They all smelled like seawater, rotting fish, and horseshit buried within a magical log house. That's how he imagined Enoch's Seattle: the dreams and the bodies.

·   ·   ·   ·   ·

The green fields surrounding St. Brendan's came into view and the stony edifice amidst the grass and shrubs opened its grey arms around the horizon. Nearing the psychiatric asylum's front courtyard, the doctor saw a smallish man in a black suit pacing in front of the large oak doors which marked the building's entrance. The coach rolled to a stop and the doctor popped the compartment door and laid his cane out the cab before his foot.

John O'Connor Donelan[1] threw out his hand to assist the doctor, but Dooley shooed the medical superintendent's away with the handle of his cane.

"No John, this is my exercise for the day."

"I see so, but are ye sure you're not over doing it?"

John's smile didn't lighten the doctor's mood and so he dropped it and moved on.

"A surprise having you here, Thom," he said. "I can assure you everyone's health in the building is right—I've seen no signs of consumption—"

"I don't care much how clean you keep your patients, Donelan!" Dooley said. "I'm here to speak with you and visit Ashling Cowen."

Donelan shook his head and then swept his hand across his bald spot. He looked up at Dooley and wondered if the man was drunk; he was a pleasant enough man until the drink was in him.

"Under what authority do you propose to see her?"

Dooley softened his eyes and relaxed his jaw.

"It's a doctor's curiosity, John," he said. "That, and the fact I've come into possession of something strange and I want to see if it connects to the murders."

Donelan raised his chin and peered over Dooley's head to the coachman who sat waiting for orders. The superintendent took one hand from his pocket and motioned the driver to circle and park along the side of the asylum. Dooley nodded to Donelan, but Donelan didn't notice because his gaze was fixed upon the horizon, deep in his own thoughts. Dooley noticed and it bothered him.

●   ●   ●   ●   ●

The girl was small, her eyelids dimmed under the weight of sedation. She lay on her side, her knees pushed into her stomach. Her hands were clasped, the matted ball of fingers rested beside her face. The sun's last rays of the day slipped from the room and made it dark. Dooley asked for a lamp. Ashling didn't react to his presence or Donelan's assurance he was a good man. Dooley shuffled to the bed, pursing his lips for want of a drink, and rested his hands on the steel bed frame. She tensed up and he let go, she relaxed again. Dooley walked to the other side of the bed and blocked her eyes from the window. She blinked. Dooley eyed Donelan as if lost for words. He asked the girl if she killed her father.

"No."

Dooley sighed and asked the orderly for a chair.

"The RIC thinks you did."

She didn't respond.

Donelan looked at Dooley and wondered what the doctor was in possession of which led him to Ashling Cowan.

"Do you know Mary Price?" Dooley asked. "Kathryn Foley? Emma Mulvagh?"

The girl lifted her eyes to meet Dooley's.

"No."

She rolled to her other side, turning her back on Dooley. He stood up and walked to the other side of the bed. Donelan's eyes followed the doctor.

"I think you did know Mary,' Dooley said. "You girls are from the same neighborhood, the same age."

"I didn't know a Mary Price," she said.

"Now how am I to believe two girls the same age from the Liberties never met each other? What are the chances, Ms. Cowan?"

"It's just the way it is, you stupid man."

Donelan nodded to hide his grin. Dooley was not impressed with either the girl or the superintendent.

"So, you killed your father on your own then?" Dooley said. "You just decided one night you'd take a hammer and pulverize your father's skull until all that remained were fragments of bone and bits of brain?"

"Thom!" Donelan said.

The girl squirmed and made an awful cry.

"You caved in your father's head, and the whole time blood spraying onto your nightgown, face, chest and arms; you hammered until you were too tired to lift it again and then you carried it back to your bed and laid with it until you heard your wee brother's screams in the morning?"

Donelan stood up from his chair, "Thom, I must—"

"And, you did this act alone? You copied what you heard in the papers about the other lasses doing the same to their fathers?"

Dooley ceased and a terrible silence filled the cold room. The girl sobbed and began to mumble a prayer.

"I think it was a pact between you gilpies—you daughters of hures from the Liberties. You hated your useless fathers and the hellicat covenant you formed gave you strength to carry out your evil spells."

"For Christ sake, Thom, listen to yourself," Donelan said. "You better go."

Ashling cried out again.

Dooley wheeled round, his face tight up against Donelan's, spittle speckling his lips.

"Another feckless Paddy I have to explain the obvious to," Dooley said. "Do you think just letting the lass lay in bed all day sedated is going to get you your confession?"

"Now, Thom—"

"Now, exactly. Now's when we get the truth. When we hear what these little witches did to their fathers."

"Thom, if you would let me…"

"Not a word from any of the girls. You all just let them sit and sulk when you should be pounding the truth out, pounding…"

Dooley's composure was gloved by his rage and Donelan made his way to the door for help from the orderlies. The girl shook and continued to pray.

"You stop right there, John."

Donelan stopped at the door and turned.

"What has the girl told you?"

"If you would have let me introduce what information was already acquired you would have known that—"

"It was the devil. A Scottish devil. You're all devils," she said.

Dooley whipped around.

"Who's the devil besides me?" He said.

"Yer man who made me watch'em take ma dad's head off."

"What else?" Dooley said.

"He dressed fine, like. Black suit, beaver hat. He was older, but seemed young. He tied us up. I thought he'd already killed my brother, Jackie. He said he was an angel. Nothing he said made sense. He said he was sorry. He said he wished there was a better way, but "killing our lives" like was how to get the people primed."

"Primed?" Dooley said. The redness now leached from his face.

"Scared." She kept her eyes lock on Dooley's.

"Thom, I'm going to have to ask you to leave now," Donelan said.

"What else? What else, lassie," Dooley said.

"There was blood. So much blood," she wept, her eyes full of tears. "And when he was finished he pulled a case from his jacket pocket and gave me a shot."

"A shot?"

"Opium," Donelan sighed.

Dooley kept his gaze on Donelan as the wheels turned in his head. "And then?"

"Just nightmares. The man in the black suit coming out of the shadows and chasing me with a hammer."

Ashling threw the covers over her and shook while she cried in her cocoon.

"He a Scotsman, you said?"

"Yes, Thom," Donelan said. "Now get out or I'll throw you out."

The men left the room. Donelan was shaking.

Dooley felt wrong for bullying her, but he needed to know the details. He waited to speak until they approached the exit.

"What do you think, John?" He said.

"Fenians."

"Fenians? Are you mad?"

"You heard her. The killings are a diversion. You're not blind to the unrest growing, are you? After all, you still treat Plunkett's lungs, do you not?"

"And for that, he should divulge unto me his plots against the Crown?"

"There've been rumors, Thom."

"Of what? Pickpockets stealing constables' batons?"

"Of bloodshed."

"The Fenians, as feckless and misguided as they may be, aren't daft enough to engage in a plot of patricide to mislead the RIC, or smart enough to engineer something like this."

"Then what, Thom?" Donelan said, his patience with the old drunk nearing the end of its line. "What do you propose?"

"Just what she said: a Scottish Devil."

Donelan looked at him with icy eyes, but Dooley's face was serious enough to melt them.

"So, hell has ruptured the earth's surface here in Dublin, Thom?"

"Don't be daft, John," Dooley said, and smiled. "No, the Devil took a boat over from America."

"I suppose that makes more sense," Donelan said. "And, what's this about some information you have about the killings?"

"The Devil himself sent me a confession."

"Jesus, Thom, make some sense please."

"This is not the killer's first round of murders," he said, "and I used to know him when I was in Glasgow."

"Why send anything to you?" Donelan said.

"I don't know, John," he said, "but cleansing the world's a wearisome business. I think he's sick of it and wants to be caught."

"Has he said as much? You need to take this information to the RIC."

"Aye, in good time," Dooley said. "I have to finish his book first."

They stood silent in the foyer for a moment, reclaiming their composure. Dooley continued:

"Have you checked if the other girls have stick marks on the arm?"

"No Thom, please let me know what you find, but never call me Paddy again. You're the outsider here in Dublin, and don't you forget it."

"Forgive me, friend," Dooley said.

Donelan opened the front door and whistled for Dooley's coach, but the coachman abandoned the doctor.

Xi

The tavern stank of ale-soaked floorboards, tobacco smoke and burnt oil. Four dirty lamps on the bar cast a mischievous veil over the faces of the tavern's patrons. I was inside the mouth of Skid Road—beside the Lava Beds, adjacent to the opium dens and within a stone's throw of everything else considered morally bankrupt in Seattle. I sat at the bar and ordered a whisky. Behind me three hazy faces coughed out sensationalized versions of this afternoon's public drowning. The barkeep set a glass in front of me and filled it to the brim.

"You the Scottish gentleman people been talking about?"

"No, I'm not James Colman," I said, a bit irritated with the attention.

"Funny. No, you're the guy who's shown up when all the murders happened—what a coincidence."

"That I'm here?"

"No, that you were there," he said.

He stared at me while fixing the cork back into the bottle and then turned away to gesticulate he was going to keep an eye on me. Besides his lopsided mustache and receding hairline there was no other reason to pay attention to him. He walked away from the bar and disappeared behind a heavy red curtain.

I heard the voices behind me go quiet. When they picked back up it was in Native jargon. I presumed they were talking about me. However, it didn't take long until they were speaking English again.

"You think he'd cut off his own hand? Naw now, I reckon things happened how he said they did."

"He just did it to make it look like he ain't the killer."

"But I heard the killer threw the girl's daddy's body from the roof while he was in the alley with Butterfield."

"Might be two of them then for all we know."

"Could be him and that whore, Lou Graham."

I turned around and held up my bandaged stump from its sling in front of me.

"I can assure you I don't have what it takes to cut off my own hand to save face. And, even if I did, I'd choosing something a little more civilized than a stable door."

The audience of silhouettes sat motionless until one picked up his mug of ale and took a long drink before slamming it back onto the table. I turned back to my whisky and took the lot of it to match.

The barkeep came back and gave a look to the party behind me and then to me.

"See you were making friends while I was gone."

"I wouldn't call it that."

"I'd say you're in a mighty rough part of town to be spoutin' off," he said, without taking his eyes off the glass he was drying. "Maybe you should head up to the hotels; they've got plenty of whisky and more of your sort."

"Aye?"

"I?"

I felt the whisky warm my blood and I wasn't feeling polite.

"I, what?" he asked again.

"Aye, I would like another whisky."

"I don't think so."

"And why not…"

I heard the steps from behind, but I didn't have time to turn around when the barkeep burst into a cloud of Chinese rockets and gold dust. Shards of glass glowed from the sparks and reflected every broken idea I could fathom before I slipped from my stool and onto the floor. I sat slouched on the ground with my back resting on the Bar's foot pedals. Hovering over me were three ghosts dangling like they didn't know what to do next. The pain came and the hammering was intense. Wetness came down my face and I wondered why they were pouring water on me; I didn't realize it was my own blood flowing down my face. I muttered something and they laughed. They laughed and I wanted to kill them for it. I tried to pick myself up but couldn't and they laughed even more. Then, I heard glass break, and when it did the room grew dim. I heard another smash and the tavern grew even dimmer. The barkeep and my attackers began to yell, and then there came two more crashes and the tavern was dark. Screams tore through the darkness, a clatter of feet, and the sound of splitting wood, or perhaps breaking bones. The whines of men becoming boys was pathetic, but relatable. I lost consciousness and retired to my own dark room wondering if I'd be killed next. Fear.

Xii

When I was a child in Glasgow I used to be able to see Ben Lomond[li] on a clear day from my father's office window. It was not often but when he was free he told me stories of the Highlanders who lived above the city. Tales of the Highland caterans[lii] stealing livestock for blackmail and tales of Rob Roy MacGregor's[liii] blood feud against the Duke of Montrose.[liv] I looked at the dim outline of the mountain as he recited the long list of events which led to both the Stuart Rebellions.[lv] And when he was done with those stories we looked down onto the city and he told me about the riots against Scotland's Union with England[lvi] and the Malt Tax Riots.[lvii]

He said long ago our family were Highlanders, but not anymore, no matter what my grandfather and uncle said. He said we were outlaws, but at a time when most men were. Back then there was enough lawlessness going around between those abusing their powers and the malnourished, it was pointless pointing fingers at people from so long ago. Ben Lomond and the city below it held these stories.

When I was a few years older a factory was erected next to my father's office and blocked our view of the Highlands. Ben Lomond was gone and Glasgow was too for that matter because all we could see out of the window was a wall of stones.

"They brought the Highlands closer to us," Father said, to console me the first time I saw the view erased, "all this stone and mortar is from there."

His words didn't console me. I recall it was about this time I stopped daydreaming about the Highlands, what my ancestors might have looked like, and of Rob Roy. The tall buildings kept my eyes turned inwards, when maybe lang syne the vastness of Scotland's countryside made men more contemplative of their relationship with the wild. Our summer visits to the Isle of Skye never made me feel that way. I remember my feet always being wet, and shivering in bed with little more than a sheet to keep me warm.

Upon my first break from university I visited our new country home in Bearsden. The white-capped Ben Lomond was framed inside a windowpane rising above my father's desk in his study. It meant nothing to me, but it did to him and so I smiled and said to him he did the right thing to move Mother away from the wretched smoke of the city for a while. Twenty years was too long in one place and Bessy, our old castle, had become a prison. Unfortunately, we returned to our prison as often people do.

Xiii

She jumped off the cliff again and I watch her break apart on the sea
rocks below like a wooden ship gone aground. It's the bloody
currents of the ocean. The bloody currents cannot be controlled when
you sail too close to shore.
I'm pushed in the back and falling. I wished to be an albatross to
be far from the clutch of the current.
Drowning, inflated black lungs rise to the surface.
I sink instead and look for her despite what I know —
There, underneath the waves, is Wahalchoo's longhouse.

SHE IS NOT THERE.

Xiv

I came to gasping for air, thinking I was on the floor of the tavern with lungs full of kelp. Instead, I was in a small shanty. The roof was pasted with canvas stretched over lengths of withered driftwood. The walls were a collage of lumber ends, wooden boards and rusty tin ceiling tiles. A lantern hung on a nail against the far wall and illuminated a man slumped on a chair with a hat over his face. He was asleep. I was lying on a mattress. I looked around to investigate where the sound of running water came from and saw a skinny stream run through the middle of the hovel's mud floor. The water flowed toward the shack's fly-door and out onto the street. I had no idea where I was or how I got there, but I wanted to leave. My head was a sandbag.

"How did I get here?" I said.

The sleeping man didn't stir.

"How did I get here? Wake up."

I tried to answer my own question, but nothing developed in my memory except a catalogue of faces. Lou. Chief Butterfield. Colman. Dr. Tom. Burke. The dead boy pulled from the sinkhole. The pig's head. Furth. McGilvra's assistant, Charles. Anna. Mr. Richards. His eye. Princess Angeline. Mother. The concierge at the Brunswick Hotel and his twin. The girl. The smudged face of the killer. Flies. The barkeep. Her. The longhouse. My thoughts were unspooling—coming undone.

"Wake up!"

The man stirred.

"Sleep," he grumbled.

"Who are you?"

"Sleep. I'm nobody."

"How did I get here?"

"I carried you here."

"What happened?"

No response.

"Talk to me," I said.

"There are dead men," he said, sounding hesitant.

"Where?"

"The tavern."

"I don't understand. Why did you bring me here?"

"He made me."

"Who?"

The man rolled over.

"A young man. Looked like police. He gave me money and said if I refused he would kill me."

"What young man?"

"A white man."

He got up, walked to the bed and stood over me. He had blood on him. Strands of black hair lay wet and pasted against his face. He was an Indian.

"You have blood on you," I said.

"Your blood."

"I see. You're an Indian."

"You have a terrible voice," he said in response.

"I'm from Scotland."

"In England."

"Above England."

"But, you are English?"

"No, but you would not understand," I said.

"Because I am an Indian? My teachers in the boarding schools said you were the same. Up north there are many English."

"They would tell you that, but we're different."

"I don't see how."

"Just from a different place."

The man turned and went to the far corner underneath the lantern and dug through a canvas bag and pulled out a tattered envelope then returned to the side of the bed.

"This is my wife. She's in Vancouver with her family. She works in an English home while I'm down here working in Mr. Yesler's mill. We are different people than the ones down here. Is that what you mean."

"Yes."

The photograph was weathered and creased. The man and his wife stood together in a suit and white dress. It was their wedding picture. I did not know what I was supposed to say other than thank you.

"What is your name?" I asked.

"Robert."

He scanned the canvas roof and saw a bulge of rainwater had pooled and pushed the sagging area with a forceful heave.

"Why don't you live in one of Yesler's boarding houses if you work for him?"

"They're full."

"It's miserable to live outside."

"Sometimes, but it's more miserable to live away from your family."

"Sometimes."

He looked at me.

"What did the man who paid you look like?" I continued.

"It was dark and his mouth was covered with a scarf. He was out of breath. He was young. Wore police boots."

"Perhaps the killer?"

"Maybe so."

We considered each other for a while to try and find something else in common. We were both outsiders, but with circumstances quite different. His house, if you wanted to call it that, had no consistency in its construction; it was built with the material leftovers of other structures more uniform and exact. However, Robert appeared to have a goal, something which made living like that okay; even if the goal was to make enough money to leave and return home to his wife.

"Do you know him?" Robert asked.

"No. Or, at least I don't think so."

"He said you were his friend."

"Ni."

"He kills children."

"Why we're not friends," I said.

"Who is he?"

"I don't know." Princess Angeline reappeared in my mind. "Who's princess Angeline?"

"That's a strange question. You're asking because I'm an Indian?"

"I suppose."

"She's Chief Seeathl's daughter," he said.

"Whom Seattle is named after?"

"Yes. A rich white woman named her Princess Angeline because she thought it sounded prettier than her real name. She lives to the north along the beach."

"What's her real name?"

"Kikisoblu."

"I saw her there."

"Where?"

"Along the beach."

Robert knelt beside me. He was lean and his shoulders were broad and powerful, but his eyes were sunken. He was overworked.

"What were you doing there? There's nobody but Indians," he said.

"I was following somebody."

"That's your business," he said. "I know Angeline is very old. She washes clothes and makes baskets."

"She said to come back when I have clothes needing washing."

Robert scanned my bloodstained shirt and coat.

"You look dirty to me."

I looked down at myself.

"Indeed, I am."

Robert turned away from me and put away his wedding photo.

"Maybe you should go, there's no room here," he said.

"Did you build this, Robert?"

He scanned the waterlogged canvas ceiling.

"It was someone else's before, but he abandoned it, so it's mine now."

I saw a pile of tin cups and pots heaped together at the foot of the bed.

"Why do you collect these?" I pointed to the tin.

"They can be mended."

Then I noticed everything holding up the house and decorating it was broken. Pots, pans, a saddle, splintered signs, and canvas bags—

each one featured a broken strap or contained a hole.

"Do you sell these when they're fixed?"

"I can trade them to other workers for things, but that's it."

"What do you trade for?"

"Food, clothes."

"You don't seem like an Indian."

"How would you know?"

"Fair enough."

"I was raised in a boarding school. I speak English and broken pieces of Kwak'wala."[lviii]

"That's the language of your people?"

"I have no people."

"They're dead?"

"No, I'm not Indian enough or English enough," he said, irritated. "Can you stand?"

"I don't think so," I said.

"I can walk with you. Where do you live?"

"Madam Lou's."

"The brothel?"

"Yes."

"What's your name?"

"Enoch."

"What does it mean?"

"He was the grandfather of Noah, from the bible."

"And what did he do? I don't remember him."

"He walked in heaven and watched the angels fall."[lix]

XV

It was late. Small fires burned and stray bodies stumbled up and down Mill Street. Robert helped me stand with his hand around my waist and pulled me towards his body. We reached 2nd Avenue and turned left towards Lou's, but the road was occupied with police. He tried to turn us around, but a series of shouts sprang forth and we were spotted. They ran towards us and Robert stood fast even though I told him he should run. He said he didn't do anything. We were wrestled from each other and restrained. I was held with my hands pinned behind my back and received a jab to my stomach and fell to my knees. The side of Robert's face was pushed into the mud and a short stocky man without a police uniform sunk his boot into Robert's back.

From my knees I lurched forward, but my hair was grabbed before I fell on my face. Chief Butterfield walked into the middle of the confusion and asked for Robert's name, but he refused to speak. There was a crowd of uniforms around us, licking their chops.

"You're in trouble now, Enoch," Butterfield said.

"I'm hurt," was all I could manage.

"I could care less," Butterfield shouted. "Unless you can tell me why I have four dead men in a tavern and another one with his face splattered all over the entrance to Yesler's Wharf?"

"I don't know. I was at the tavern and was hit in the head. I heard yelling but blacked out before I could see what happened."

"I have a witness who saw this Indian carry you out of the tavern."

"I was outside when he gave him to me," Robert said.

"What the hell is that supposed to mean?"

"The killer forced Robert to carry me," I said.

"The bodies in the tavern are all cut up. Not our killer; just another fight gone too far."

"It was him."

Butterfield ignored me.

"What does the Indian have to say for himself?" Butterfield turned his attention to Robert, who was still pinned to the earth.

"The man said to take his friend somewhere safe or he'd kill me."

Chief Butterfield noticed the blood on Robert's outstretched hand, and on his collar.

"An Indian with good English. So, you'll understand me when I ask where all this blood came from?"

The policemen began to swing amongst each other and murmur.

"It's his blood," Robert said, nodding his head in my direction.

"Not too fond of white men much, Robert? Were those boys in the tavern harassing you?"

"No sir. I didn't go in."

"That mess in the tavern looks like maybe you drank too much and got carried away."

"What's this, Butterfield?" I said.

A hand from behind pushed my head forward and stuffed my face in the ground. I was pulled up and Butterfield scowled at me. He'd already made up his mind about tonight.

"If you know what's good for you, keep your mouth shut."

Butterfield stepped around to the other side of Robert and knelt by him.

"You killed the men in the bar, didn't you? And then, still having the taste of blood in your mouth, waited for the first lone man to walk by along the wharf, and then you finished your night properly, in the same way as you've done with the others. Just admit it, son."

"Sure, whatever you say, police."

"This's a setup," I said.

"Take him away."

Robert was picked up and pushed down the street while the remaining officers, Butterfield and myself, watched.

"He wasn't involved," I said.

"Like hell he wasn't. If he was with you, then he was involved." Butterfield asked his officers to pick me up. We were face to face now. Butterfield's mouth was pinched with whisky and sour cigar. "I'm beginning to think you're more involved than you're leading on, son; things aren't adding up here and I think it's your doing."

"You're going about this all wrong. Neither of us are your man."

"I've got a man lying dead with his face ripped off on Main Street. I've got four bodies with slit throats bleeding out in a tavern and a witness placing you and an angry Indian there. So, you tell me who my man is, the sickly Scotsman with one hand or the able-bodied Indian who carried him away?"

"Witness?" I asked.

"One of my own officers."

"Who?" I said. "Robert said the killer wore police boots."

"One of mine that's too loyal to lie and too weak and dumb to kill four men."

"The killer's still loose," I said.

Butterfield snorted.

"I suppose if I let you go, he might be. I reckon you and the Indian are in this together."

His look was cold. However, I knew something was off because he trembled like he was afraid. I wasn't buying his stone act. He was carrying out orders.

"What's going on, Butterfield?"

He broke eye contact and looked down the street to the wharf.

"Escort him back to Lou's," he ordered. "God knows whose blood is on you, but get cleaned up, Enoch. You're lucky I'm not arresting you; we got one, and that will satisfy the papers and the public for now."

"You can't be—"

"Not another word or I'm charging you with murder."

A thorny feeling spiked my insides. I was worried, worried about Robert. An ulcer. Myself be damned. A black rose.

Xvi

Out of all of Butterfield's officers, the greenest of the lot, Joshua Foley, escorted me back to Lou's. He was dark haired, trim, blue-eyed, and out of uniform. His features were sharp, but he gave me the feeling like he was lost in his own shoes. He said his grandfather was from Ireland and he was Irish too. I couldn't detect his accent. Like most yanks, they all sound American, but say they're from somewhere else. I can't fathom it, but I suppose the missing link to home hurts through the generations—I couldn't say.

"Is it as green as they say?"

"No greener than many parts of Scotland," I responded.

"Is the Burren as rocky as they say?"

"Not any more so than the Highland peaks."

"Aren't you Irish?" he asked.

"I'm Scottish."

He looked away.

"I thought you were Irish."

"We sound nothing alike," I said.

"You do to me."

We approached the front door and I felt a tug towards the wharf. The body was somehow connected to Butterfield. Foley appeared desperate, like the body was an ill omen, an end of something. I envisioned the blood splattered on the victim's suit. I saw what he looked like before—old and ugly. I needed to know who he was; the pull was too great to ignore.

We arrived at Lou's front door. The bar was dark and empty. Only the lamps beside the stairwell were lit.

"Thank you," I said, "but, I can take it from here."

"I was told to escort you to your room, sir."

"No need."

"But, it was an order," he said, cowering a little.

"Then you realize what you're entering, don't you?"

"Sir?"

"This is a brothel. All the couples have retired upstairs to their rooms. What would your mother think of you passing by those doors? A good Catholic boy, like yourself?"

"Well, I don't have—"

"Aye, but you know the chances of you getting out are quite slim here?"

"I haven't the—"

"I have nowhere else to go but to my room. If you would prefer to listen to the endless sounds of creaking bed springs and the sinful wailings of fornication and adultery by all means take the extra fifteen steps up the stairs to tuck me into bed."

"Is it that loud?"

"If you can imagine an infirmary full of patients dying of plague, but enjoying it, that's the closest I can think of."

"If you promise, I'll leave you here."

"As I said, where else would I go at this time?"

He walked away, but then turned around to see if I entered.

"I saw you," he said, a horrific smile on his face. He turned and ran off. Saw me where?

I pushed open the door and put half my body inside it and waited for the curious young officer to turn the corner. When he did I tucked back outside and closed the glass-paneled door behind me to see Anna at the foot of the stairs. She stared. I knew it was a mistake to leave, but I hadn't the sense to stay. I shrugged my shoulders and then turned and stepped off the porch. I hoped there was some big truth lying on the street that would cleanse my mistake.

•　　•　　•　　•　　•

The body laid in the street sixty feet from me. I was behind a horseless coach in a dark recess. Yesler was there wrapped in a black cape. He peered down at the dead man and then stepped back and turned to look at the front entrance to his mill. Butterfield walked over to him and whispered something in his ear while Doctor Tom bent over the body. It was hard to tell, but the victim's face didn't appear disfigured. The doctor stood up and turned his back to the body while stuffing his hand into his coat pocket and producing his little box of white powder. He dipped his finger into it and then pushed it up into his nostril. In my mind, I saw the dead girl's father fall from the sky and land in the alley again; the look on Dr. Tom's face took me back to the chase and to the door that severed my hand. Yet, this scene didn't feel the same; it didn't possess the same confidence the other killings did.

Every time a gust of wind leapt from the bay, the doctor, Butterfield, and his men stretched and shuddered with the lamplight. However, Yesler stayed still as stone as if he were anchored deep into the earth. Thomas Burke appeared out of the coach near them, and inside was one more person, but I couldn't tell who. Burke stood next to Yesler and they looked down at the body like two boys who'd broken a window.

I turned to walk around the block and investigate the scene from the other side, but was surprised by Mr. Richards. He was drunk and smelled of sex.

"What're ya doin', huh?" he slurred, "what're ya lookin' at?"

"Mr. Richards, what are you doing about?" I said.

"Might ask ya the same thin'. Goin' home."

"Lou's curfew passed an hour ago."

"Just came from there. Sweet young woman you might know?"

Richards swayed and his dead eye rolled around in its socket. He hunched over and peered towards the body and began to laugh. I could have punched him.

"Is that ol' Yesler himself? Well I can't believe he'd be out this late."

"It's a body."

"A whatee?"

"They found another body," I repeated.

He took his time searching.

"I dinna see na body on the ground. I'll go talk to Yesler and Butterfield about seeing ya spying on'em. Make you look'n guilty don't it too?"

"I've already talked to Butterfield. They arrested an Indian."

"Good. Knew 'twas an Indian from the start."

I tried to keep him from leaving, but I couldn't. He staggered towards Butterfield and his officers and walked right up to the body, giving it a long look, while Butterfield, Yesler and Burke did the same to him. Richards shared a word with them. I couldn't hear a thing, but none of them turned my way to indicate Richards had informed them of my presence. After another minute, Richards shook his head, waved them good night, and walked back towards me, but passed without acknowledging my presence.

I saw Butterfield shaking hands with Yesler and Burke. Together they looked up the street and I figured then I was caught. Roberts must have mentioned my presence after all. Butterfield appointed two policemen to engage and I fought the urge to run because my head hurt too much. I placed myself in the dark ribbon between the coach and the street and awaited their arrival. I looked up the street and watched Richard disappear into the darkness. The clomping boots neared. The officers arrived, but passed me. It didn't make sense, if not to capture me, I wondered where the two policemen were going?

I turned back to the body. The party of men stood around waiting for something. Another ten minutes went by until an officer appeared with a bolt of canvas tucked under his arm. He and two others wrapped the body in the rigid material and then tied the corpse's legs, torso and neck with rope before rolling it to the edge of the wharf. I risked it and crept closer to the next shadowy recess. I saw a canoe approach the wharf. It disappeared under the height of the harbor, but was headed to shore. The two officers picked up the bundle and lowered it towards the four hands raised from the obscured canoe. Butterfield, Dr. Tom, Burke and Yesler oversaw the transfer and as the slim vessel set off, back into the wet-night of the bay, they walked away together and climbed into the coach. Butterfield's officers extinguished their lanterns and meandered up Mill Street.

Dublin, 1916

It was Good Friday and Dr. Dooley roused from his cupped mattress and staggered to the loo like his room were a small boat at sea. He returned and sat on his bed and peered down at the hairless folds of his belly. His guts were full of acid and his cranium, a well of stress. He'd returned late into the city centre from the sanitarium, and read Enoch's manuscript into the wee hours. The strangeness of the girl's story didn't bothered him, but knowing the killer was a Scotsman, did. Now, it was reasonable to suspect the killer was writing him and entangling him in a very dangerous game.

Dooley went over to his desk and flipped through what he read the night before. Bar fights, a strange passage about Ben Lomond, and even stranger nonsense about an Indian cabin and a drowned boy. Not to mention the story of an Indian killer and a dead body dropped into a canoe and paddled away. With every page, Enoch's story sounded more like fantasy. Was Enoch's story merely the hallucinations of a madman, or an elucidation of strange facts told by a man troubled by his past? All Dooley had to rely on was Enoch's own words—a narrative that points the finger to a homicidal philosopher and a grand conspiracy.

Dooley knew Enoch sent the manuscript within Ireland, most likely Dublin. The girl called her father's killer a Scottish devil. These details weren't proof, but they pointed to Enoch. He could be the killer. Dooley couldn't make up his mind. Enoch's proof of innocence was too circumstantial, and his guilt hidden in the psychological recesses of his meandering narrative.

Dooley pulled the cord for the maid before remembering she wasn't there. He wanted a cup of tea, but didn't want to go through the trouble of preparing it. He felt pathetic. He shaved to cut away his failings, and dressed himself in clean clothes to hide his shame. In turn, he spiritually undressed himself in the mirror. His face was distorted by the mirror's oxidized tin backing. He was old and unhealthy, like the city he lived in. He sighed and tied his tie while imagining Enoch's Seattle.

Dirt streets, rows of decrepit wood buildings surrounding the odd modern one. The discord of shabbiness and opulence was beyond the doctor's comprehension. He thought of Enoch's descriptions of the city as dubious. A city made up of people either rich or poor, with no one in the middle—which category was Enoch in then if the ranks within Seattle were an either-or? Black and white? Were both Enoch and the killer the only two outsiders in a city comprised of outsiders? Not probable either. Mr. Enoch Campbell appeared to be as unreliable a narrator as the editor to Hoggs' *Justified Sinner*[lx], and in suit used his title and education to legitimize his bias. Dooley stared into the mirror. He was aware he was an unhealthy doctor. He thought about his own stories and how unreliable they were.

It was bollocks, the lot of stupid shite he just thought, the grumblings of a lonely old man and a pathetic drunk. He's better at insulting people than saving them, he thought. He closed his eyes and took a deep breath before re-opening them and looking back into the mirror with confidence. "Truth restored," he said out loud. Still, his personal shame didn't excuse the fact Enoch might be the killer. They're wretches, he thought, second-rate professionals, and worse, bad liars. But nonetheless, it's hard to tell good stories, and Enoch's story, of being one of two outsiders in Seattle, wasn't necessarily at odds with his own sulk-story of being the sole Scotsman in Dublin. In fact, there are more than two, and the killer could be the third.

He turned away from the mirror dressed and ready to go.

•　　　•　　　•　　　•　　　•

"How many Scotsmen do you reckon live in Dublin?"

"What on earth kind of question is that?" Cormac responded.

The round journalist lifted his fingers from his typewriter and eyed Dooley with an expression of bewilderment and annoyance.

"Your killer is Scottish," Dooley said.

"Did you have a pint with him last night?"

The newsroom chirped with chattering keys and margin bells. The rows of oak desks were choked with papers and occupied by porter-gutted men full of strong opinions.

"So, you don't think it's the girls either?"

"I'm travelling down your road," Cormac said. "I'm not sure of anything, but you said a killer, not killers."

"So the logic follows—"

"So it follows. "

"I spoke to one of the lasses at the sanitarium yesterday. She said it was a Scottish devil who killed her father."

"Bloody hell," Cormac said.

"She said the bastard tied her and her brother up and then gave her a shot of opium."

"You're having a laugh?" Cormac said.

"We need to find out if the other girls have needle marks on them."

"I can make a few stops."

"If she's not lying about that, she might be telling the truth about the whole thing," Dooley said.

"What about the brother?"

"Coma."

"The drugs?"

"Could be. On my way to find out."

Cormac sat back in his chair and put his hands behind his head.

"I'll go find out about the marks; I've sources in the gaol."

"Right" Dooley said, "You'll call in tonight and let me know what you find?"

"I can," Cormac eyed Dooley. "No protest?"

"What you mean?"

"I've never in the years I've known you witnessed ye acquiesce to any man."

"Truth be told, I couldn't be arsed and wanted you to go. I hate gaol hospitals anyway."

"Says the doctor—"

"Says the doctor," Dooley repeated.

Cormac let out a stiff laugh.

"Regardless, Thom, all this on the record?"

"I don't know. If you're asking me if I'm a source, the answer's no."

"Well, what good is this information if I can't use it?"

Several of the men in the newsroom looked up from their typewriters. Dooley ducked his head in closer to Cormac.

"Just say it's a reputable source that led you to check out the girls at the gaol. I'll stand up to it at the end of the day if it comes down to it. I just don't want any attention from the man with the hammer. I don't have much proof right now anyway."

"For now," Cormac said. "If I make the connection myself that the boy and the girls all have a needle mark I'll print, otherwise, I'm not typing a word."

"That's your business."

"And, what's your business with this?"

"Not yours," Dooley said.

"Jesus, Thom. You better not be sticking your nose in where it doesn't belong?"

"I didn't want to be involved," Dooley said, walking away. "But, you know Scotsmen, if you don't write about it to someone, it never happened."

Confused, Cormac mouthed Dooley's words back to himself and then like a switch, stood up from his seat.

"The fecker's writing to you?"

There was a momentary silence in the newsroom as the reporters turned to watch the doctor exit. Dooley topped his hat without turning and vanished through the stairwell.

•   •   •   •   •

Cormac stepped off the footpath, onto the slick cobble in front of 31 Westmoreland Street[lxi], and looked left toward the old parliament and Trinity College.[lxii] It was night and the lights ricocheted off the wet streets. He needed to hail a taxi for the gaol. Much to his luck and surprise a coach pulled beside him and the coachman, in a wet-velvety Wicklow accent, asked if he needed a lift. Cormac waved him off from assisting him into the coach, and when he was settled banged on its side to signal he was ready. It began its bumpy jaunt towards the girls, their needle marks, and the lead he hoped would break his story onto the front page.

The cobble-bop of the road bounced Cormac's head into a sweet sleepy rhythm, and he was almost fast asleep when the coach came to a stop. He sat motionless in the dark box feeling ill at ease. He smelled tobacco and heard two feet hit the cobbles. They approached the coach door and there came a knock.

"Sorry, sir," the coachman said. "I need to ask ye something."

"No bother," Cormac said.

"Can ye open the door?"

Cormac opened the door and the coachman climbed in. They sat in the darkness. Cormac couldn't make out the coachman's face on account he wore a dark scarf over his nose and mouth.

"What's this about?" Cormac said.

"Why does he have you going to the gaol?"

"My errand is my business."

The coachman leaned closer to Cormac.

"You're in no position to be a big man. Now, why're you going to the gaol?"

Cormac tried to speak, but nothing came out. He swallowed to lubricate his throat. He knew he was in danger.

"Come on, out with it!"

"Are you a Yank?" Cormac asked, detecting a drop in the coachman's accent.

"Last chance. Why are you going to the gaol?"

"A fecking Yank," Cormac said, "A fecking yank holding up an Irishman in his own country? I suppose you're the man writing to

Thom then?"

The dark silhouette retracted in his seat, slipping deeper into the shadows.

"The doctor knows who you are," Cormac said, to jolt the man and buy him some time.

"He's looking for proof, isn't he?" the coachman said.

"And a Scotsman."

"I ken, for the needle marks left on the gilpies?" the coachman said, again switching accents.

Cormac's bared his teeth like his hand was sliced. He knew he was dead and felt his blood ready to boil over.

"Are you a fecking Yank, or a Jock? A Yank base on your shite Scots."

The coachman moved like a whip and the short blade he held slipped into Cormac's fatty neck. The journalist felt the hilt punch his throat before he felt pain. He choked, and then after a moment—which appeared to the coachman like he took pause to peak out the window and contemplate his last moments—slumped in his seat. In vain, Cormac pressed his hand around the blade to slow the bleeding.

"I'll tell you everything," Cormac gasped.

The coachman watched him bleed out.

"*Felo de se,*" he said. "For being so rude to me."

Cormac expired knowing he played his hand wrong.

Xvii

Lou pounded on my door half six in the morning and the deep thuds roused me from a horrific dream. Robert hung from Yesler's scantlings and I couldn't save him because a hammer was chained to my left hand and I hadn't my right to cut him down.

"Where were you?"

"Nowhere."

"That's not good enough an answer for me," she said.

I noticed she held an envelope.

"What's that?"

"Another one of your love letters."

"Give it here."

Lou pushed her way into my room and saw the blood-soaked linens I used to clean myself last night.

"Young man, your skin is streaked with blood. Anna mentioned she saw you enter and leave here past curfew last night. And, above all this, there are bodies strewn all about the city this morning."

"Lou, I need to read the letter."

"You can read it in front of me."

"If you insist," I said.

"I insist."

She stomped from the fireplace adjacent to the bed and dropped the envelope onto my lap. It was handmade—just like the others—of bleached cardstock. I opened the parcel and the letter was the same, drafted on the same paper as before, hand written.

"Dear Enoch,

"Last night, I was not impressed with your exhibition of intemperance, and your inept understanding of basic conversational protocol with the lower classes. I did not enjoy killing them, but little you would have noticed—being you were bludgeoned into a pile—but it was a case of you or them, and I figured I owed you a favor for cutting off your hand. How is it healing?

"A lot has happened since yesterday and what a beautiful day it was. I knew beforehand there was an important secret visitor coming to town who needed to be dealt with, but the altercation at the tavern, Robert the Indian at the right place at the right time, and of course the symbolic drowning of the poor young boy, turned my intended single blood statement into a dramatic story I could never have written, or for that matter predicted. But, as you will soon find, both you and I have been victimized by the modern entrepreneurs' acute ability to harness the crimson extensions of pragmatism and subterfuge. It seems to me the City Council has time on their side, and the resources to reinvent the past.

"They indeed can invent time, and both you and I will be forced to run under the fisted hands of their clocks. However, do not be discouraged; in the master-slave relationship who needs who? And, within that vacuum, which reflection will we choose for the masters to see? This indeed is our control over the future and our laugher at work. If they don't have the masses, what do they have?

"Do you see those who are searching for the longhouse are desperate? I feel for the Indian they arrested. It seems a terrible price to pay just to teach you a lesson, but that's the point. They are the law, Enoch, and like water, justice takes the shape of the vessel it fills.

"There is an indifference to justice and how it flows. Let us watch how death will continue to spur progress, but my killing, spurn it. So, I wonder now how much more proof will you need before you realize you side with the wrong, and your hatred towards me is misplaced. All I want is for you to believe in something.

"In the coming day, there will be a series of inconsistencies I hope will haunt you. In addition, you will find the freedom they've granted you—at the expense of Robert's—further restricted. You're their prisoner and they will not let you leave now that the shallow capacity of their creativity has forged the *spread of fear and paranoia. In other words, Yesler, Burke, Colman, Furth and the rest have big plans, too big to fail, and there can be no loose ends.*

"Rest assured I'm doing my best to keep you safe in these trying times, but do yourself a favor and go back to work; it's there, within the lion's mouth, you'll be safest.

"P.S. Keep Lou in the dark. It is for hers and your own wellbeing you do so."

"What did that maniac have to say now?" Lou asked, pacing from one side of my room to the other.

"Just more philosophical nonsense and justifications."

Lou continued to pace, engrossed in another train of thought and unable to hear me.

"Lou?"

"Yes?" she said, stopping in the middle of the floor.

"What's the matter?"

"What did you see?" she asked.

"What do you mean?"

"Last night, damn it. What happened?"

I told her of the tavern, Robert, and the arrest. That after Robert was arrested I was escorted home and went to bed. She did not appear satisfied.

"Anna saw you leave. Don't lie to me, Enoch. What did you do?"

"She was mistaken," I said. "I went back out to get more information from Butterfield's escort about the murder on Mill Street, that was all."

"Anna said she stayed up for you until 4 am, but you hadn't returned."

"Lou, I don't know what to say; she must have missed me when I returned. I was no more than five minutes."

I remembered seeing her asleep on the bar when I returned, just before dawn.

Lou gave me a rotten look and I felt sick lying to her, but I did believe the killer; for her own protection there were things I couldn't share.

"If Butterfield or anyone else asks if I left after I was escorted home you tell them I was here."

Lou's sour face turned into a concerned glare. I supposed my own anxiety was proving too strong to suppress. I wanted her to read my thoughts so she could at least sympathize with my position, but it was a mistake to command her to do anything.

"You need to tell me what's going on," she said.

"I have no idea what's going on. All I know is they arrested an innocent man."

"How are you so sure?" Lou asked, folding her arms. "You were unconscious, weren't you?"

"The killer told him to take me."

"The Indian could have made the whole thing up."

"The killer told me the same in his letter."

"Let me read it."

"No."

"Why?" she said.

"It will make you part of this and put you in danger."

"I am a part of this," she said.

Lou fiddled with a large oval amulet sutured around her neck.

"No, you're still a bystander, and it should stay that way," I said.

"Seems to me anyone's involvement is up to the killer and not you."

"You may be right, and when he sends you a letter, you can read it."

"I should ring Jacob Furth around for a meeting," she said.

"No, not Furth, or Colman for that matter."

"Why?"

They're connected to whatever is going on, I thought, any one of them.

"I especially don't want Colman or my family to be worried about anything," I said.

"It's a little too late for that!" she said.

"No, I'm safe. He won't kill me."

"The Indian?"

"The killer," I said.

"Why?"

"The language of the letters and the subject matter, the philosophy, and his outsider perspective. He's a white man. American, maybe English, but not an Indian. Anyway, how could Robert be the killer and still send me a letter from his jail cell?"

"An accomplice?" she poked, unconvinced. "Then who? If not the Indian, you?"

I was thrown back. I was losing Lou's confidence now, and all because I lied to her. However, my confidence was growing. For once, I felt energetic, and a reason to fight brewed inside me.

"Lou, I know how things look, but I'm not involved."

"Sure, you are, you've been involved since you got here."

"I haven't killed anyone," I said.

"No, perhaps not," she said, "Not directly."

"Lou?"

"What did you see?" she shouted.

I was sitting on the edge of my bed and put my palm to my temple to quell the anger inside me.

"Nothing, Lou. Please don't ask again."

"Should I be worried?"

The questions tumbled down my ears and got lost.

"I'll be fine."

"I didn't mean about you. What about my girls and myself?"

"You think I'm the killer?" I said.

"It's no secret, between your past and your fascination with the killings, you enjoy death. If you are the killer or not, it seems to follow you wherever you go."

She walked to the door and stood with her back to me.

"Aye, I'll admit it's attached to me. That crossing an ocean was not drastic enough a maneuver to outrun it. But, I do not commit to it; it's not a path stone I'll step on. I've been reliving things which need to go. It's a circle."

"But you walk and trample the garden laid beside that path stone, do you not? You act as though you're the sole person who's lost someone important," Lou said, turning around. "Don't you realize everyone in this town lost something to be here?"

"You have no idea what I went through, Lou. Please leave," I said, knowing my pride misplaced my judgment.

"You do not get to tell your host to leave her lodgings."

"Then stay," I said.

"I think I'll leave," she said, after a moment.

She rushed out of the room and slammed the door and as I stood to lock it she opened it ajar.

"Take your bloody laundry somewhere else too; since this mess is none of my business, I wish not to explain to the launderer the stains."

"Fair enough. I'm sorry, Lou."

Her heels stamped down the hallway and down the stairs. The killer was right, the noose around my neck was tightening.

Xviii

I dressed and stared at the pile of bloody clothes on the floor. My shirt was the only thing worth keeping. The rusty brown hue of the dried bloody linens smelled of iron. I imagined a railway bisecting Princess Angeline's shack—the delicate bent frame of the hovel shuttering with the coastal breeze until obliterated by the passing of Seattle's first bayside railcar. Angeline asked me to return when I had dirty laundry. The next day, after so much went wrong, she was perhaps the only person able to discern my innocence beyond the blood. I left my room.

"Enoch." Anna's voice sparked when I cleared the stairs and entered the drawing room. She sat on the lounge beside the door with a heavy book laid open on her lap. She pushed an envelope inside the pages and closed the book. She appeared as tired as I felt.

"Good morning Anna. A letter from home?"

"Erm, yes. From my mother," she said. "Where did you go last night?"

"To ask the policeman who escorted me home a few more details about the murders."

"You never returned." She sounded annoyed.

"I'm sorry to have worried you."

"I told Lou."

"I know you did. She gave me quite a lashing this morning."

"Where did you go?"

"I wasn't gone more than five minutes and besides, I'm sorry, but it's none of your business. I know we're both foreigners here, but it's not as if we know each other, at least enough for you to care about my comings and goings."

Anna recoiled.

"You flatter yourself."

"It wouldn't be the first time. I am very late for work, but thank you for your concern."

She stood and stepped towards me and eyed the soiled shirt bound in a scrap of burlap.

"What's that?" she asked.

"Just a dirty shirt I'm taking to launder."

"I can take it to the laundry for you."

She reached for it.

I pulled the parcel away from her outstretched hands and they were left extended, empty and embarrassed.

"What's wrong with you?" she said.

"I'm sorry. I was attacked last night and out of sorts—the shirt is quite dirty."

"I can't fathom based on your attitude why anyone would wish to harm you?"

"I should be going," I said.

"Yes, I believe you should,"

"It's not you. I—"

"I don't care," she said.

"It's the murders, I need to clear my head."

"Then do it."

I stood bolted to the floor and felt each second increase the awkwardness of the situation.

"I'm going to work now." I walked to the door and opened it. "Have a good day," I said.

She opened her book and slipped the envelope under her thigh. The only friend I had left in Seattle was the killer.

Xix

I stepped out into the cold and clear morning. A seated drunkard with scorn-shaded features stared at me with indignation. I thought it odd. I maneuvered past him and heard him spit. I continued onto the boardwalk and several pedestrians crossed the street instead of passing me, and others spotted me approach and turned around. Last night made me famous.

The next few blocks stretched into a mile; and although I garnered my share of stares and dirty looks, they were less malicious, than sad. Indeed, the public procession peeling off from each side of the invisible bow breaking ahead of my person was weighted down with fatigue.

The paperboy I buy from saw me approach and stopped calling out the details from the front page. He shied away from me as I approached him.

"Did I make the paper today?"

"Yes sir," he replied.

The boy folded a copy and handed it to me. I set my laundry onto the ground, dug a coin from my pocket, and stood next to the boy as I read the front page. He turned the other way and held a fresh copy over his head.

"Bloodiest night in Seattle! Five dead! Butterfield catches killer!" The boy turned his chin in my direction. "Killer had an accomplice! Boy swallowed by street!"

I read on.

"In a day Seattle will not soon forget, three patrons: Jon Dearborn,

Nathaniel Cobbler, Michael Lewis, and owner, William M. Hanson were murdered last night inside of Hanson's Saloon. Despite the tragedy, new Police Chief, O.D. Butterfield reports, "The suspected killer of the four gentlemen has been apprehended. An inquiry will soon proceed concerning the deaths in the saloon, and of the suspect's potential involvement in the single murder committed after the saloon massacre." At this time, police will not release the identity of the suspect other than they have apprehended an Indian male.

"The fifth murder took place approximately an hour after the saloon massacre. Respected businessman and longtime local, Bartholomew K. Richards was murdered last night in front of Henry Yesler's mill. Without divulging the gruesome details of the crime, Butterfield said Mr. Richards' death was by the hand of none other than "Jack the Bludgeoner," as many locals are now calling the killer who has taken eight victims.

"The arrest of the Indian suspected in the saloon killings — whose character Chief Butterfield referred to as, "troubled and disgruntled"— has the city hoping Seattle's own Jack the Ripper is finally behind bars. It is with a heavy heart this publication extends their sincerest hope Mr. Richards is the killer's last victim.

"Butterfield added he believes the Indian is also responsible for the mutilations and deaths of the other victims, and he has reason to believe the suspect had an accomplice tied to the investigation. Butterfield has not yet ruled out an alternative theory, that the suspect in custody was a minor player in a more elaborate scenario concocted by another criminal still at large. He asks for every Seattleite to be patient and vigilant until charges are made.

"When pressed concerning the Scottish lawyer, Enoch Campbell's involvement in the case, Butterfield said little other than the foreigner was seen together with the suspect before he was apprehended, and is a material witness to the murders. Campbell, who arrived in Seattle just hours before the first killing, is considered a person of interested.

"Yesterday afternoon, Jacob Knight, son of Leonard and Mary Knight, drowned in front of an anxious crowd after the boy fell into a sinkhole on Front Street. The heroic efforts of the public were not enough to save the boy. He could not swim."

I looked up from the paper and felt my stomach drop into my shoes. The paperboy eyed me again and I returned the paper.

"It's a misunderstanding."

"Sure, mister," he said, and moved to the corner across the street quicker than I could pick up my laundry bag.

Panic flooded my bloodstream and the street spun in circles. Those bastards killed Richards, and the body they removed from outside Yesler's Wharf is the key.

I walked up the street and saw a different city than the wooden shanty town I moved into a week ago. There was more stone than before. A modern and opulent opera house down the street. Hotels constructed with fine masonry and inspiring wood work. Filled with granite and brass fixtures, not to mentions visitors from other cities and countries.

Still, decaying wooden buildings surrounded these monoliths of progress, and underneath them all, a rotten infrastructure. Seattle was a battered body with a redeemable face, but full of broken bones and a lesser known cancer eating away at its insides.

Through this gauntlet of industry was a pathway to make it out alive. I could sense it, but not quite see it.

A carriage stopped beside me.

Thomas Burke, who I'd met earlier the same night I lost my hand, stuck his head out of the coach window.

"Good morning," he said.

His presence sent a shiver through me.

"Good morning, Mr. Burke."

"Come into the coach; I'd like a word with you."

I felt as though I didn't have a choice so I stepped in. Furth was also inside.

"You're in a bit of trouble this morning." Furth spared me the formalities.

"Aye, it appears I am."

"And?" Burke said.

"And what?" I responded.

"Is it true?"

"Is what true?"

"Were you with the Indian?"

"I was knocked out in the saloon and came to in his tent."

They eyed each other.

"So, you have no recollection of the space in time between when you were assaulted and when you awoke in the Indian's tent?" Furth questioned.

"No."

"You're sure about this?" Furth said. He was agitated.

"Yes, what's this about?"

"You need a defense," Burke said.

"A defense?"

"If you're charged," Furth said.

"If I'm charged?"

Their eyes were locked onto mine in anticipation for more to come from my mouth, but I remained silent.

"We're here to help you," Furth added.

"Thank you, but I'll take legal advice when I'm charged."

"We hope this doesn't happen, but the decision could be up to you," said Burke.

I could see he too was nervous.

"In my experience, a suspect has little say if he or she is to be charged."

"It's a matter of evidence, Enoch," Burke said.

"What evidence?"

"Why haven't you turned in the killer's letters to Butterfield?" Furth asked.

I smiled.

"Did you receive one today?"

"Aye."

"What did it say?" Burke asked.

Furth seemed surprised and glared at Burke.

"That's my business," I said.

"This doesn't help your case," Burke said. "Withholding evidence incriminates you in the eyes of the law."

"In the City Council's eyes?" I retorted.

"Now Enoch," Furth cut in, "we're not pressuring you, and we're certainly not threatening you. But, you need to understand, that in a manner of speaking, you've gotten too cozy with the killer; and some, like Butterfield for instance, might say you've been playing both sides."

"For what reason would I?"

"That's what everyone wants to know."

"I appreciate your concern gentleman, but until I speak to Butterfield and ordered to dispense of my personal property, the letters are mine."

"You have a naïve understanding of the law, Enoch," Burke said, "and not much sense."

"We simply want to know if your intentions are pure?" Furth said. "We're trying to reason with you."

"Gentleman, I thank you, but I should be on my way."

"There's still some ambiguity concerning your whereabouts last night," Burke said.

"My missing hour?"

"Officer Foley said he dropped you at Lou's but you talked him out of accompanying you to your room. We heard you may have left again."

"I went to my room, washed my blood from my own body, and went to bed."

"We want to believe you," Furth said.

"It's as easy as that," I said.

I made for the door and stepped out, but Burke grabbed my arm.

"What did the letter say, dammit."

I pulled my arm loose and walked away.

Xμ

I entered Angeline's encampment like a wet dog in need of a kind human. The man I saw last time stood outside his small cabin and gave me a long look. He then disengaged and went on throwing seed to his chickens before he went inside his home. On her crooked porch, she sat on a short stool, her hands gripping her knees. Two large tin basins of water sat between us. Clothes hung from a line spanning from the house to a post hammered into the sand on the corner of her small property. She sat still, like she wasn't thinking of anything which had to do with the present. The stacks of half-woven reed baskets beside her insisted upon this somehow.

"So, our killer has dirty laundry," she said.

"I'm not the killer. Did you hear about the saloon incident?" I responded.

"What saloon?"

"I—It's not important, but I was attacked and need my shirt cleaned." I pulled out the bloodstained shirt and held it up.

"The blood will have to soak in the salt water," she said.

She stood up and pointed her walking stick at one of the buckets and then pointed to the shirt. She pushed open her door and walked into the dark crease.

"Come in."

I turned and saw the man with the red shirt watch us from his door. I waved, but he didn't move. I pushed open the gate and dropped my shirt into the bucket of salt water and climbed the stairs. I entered the small single room which made up the whole of her house. Beside the door lay a thin mattress without a frame. Stacked on the left side of the dim room was a hill of tin mugs and more stacks of half-woven baskets. Mounded on the other side of the room were dozens upon dozens of shells. In the middle of the floor burned a small cast-iron stove. She apologized for the strong smell of the sea. I picked up a mug to find it and all the rest were broken.

"Why do you collect broken mugs and empty shells?" I asked, remembering Robert's tent, and the stacks of broken cups he stored there.

"If the tin is shiny enough I can make them into ornaments for blankets. The shells can always be thrown back into the sea, but I like them."[lxiii]

Her house was full of what she thought she needed. She waved me to a small chair next to the bed she sat on. We sat in silence. The dim orange glow emanating from the stove seeped into her wrinkles and so I put a few more logs inside it to brighten her face.

"Your neighbor doesn't seem to care for me," I said.

She didn't respond.

"He ignores me when I come."

She took a deep breath.

"A few years ago, the measles came and swallowed his son. He was so afraid if the white settlers found out they would make the rest of his family move away. He took his dead son into the hills and stuffed him inside a tree stump."[lxiv]

I breathed through my nose the strong smell coming from her stack of shells and let it consume me to keep from showing my surprise.

"He is a tender man, but a fool," she said. "He's lucky Yesler and the rest of them realized this when they found the boy." She took in the shells through her nostrils also. "Since then, he worries someone is going to come and grab him. You might be the one."

"He's afraid?"

"Afraid of the law," she said.

I picked up a broken cup and spun it around my finger trying to think of something important.

"They arrested an Indian I met named Robert. He was in the wrong place at the wrong time and they're going to charge him for murder."

She peered down at her hands and fanned her fingers apart before she reconnected with me.

"This is not the first time this has happened."

"They have no evidence."

"He's an Indian man."

She was right.

"Do you know about Wahalchoo's longhouse?" I asked.

She laughed.

"What longhouse?"

"I was told a story about a boy a long time ago who had a dream about a longhouse in the water."

She chuckled some more and then folded her hands together. She inspected the bump on my head and the bruising around my forehead.

"I'm not certain I can take the stains out of your shirt. Is it your blood?"

"Yes."

She nodded, but didn't say anything. We stayed silent until she decided to speak.

"There's a killer here in Seattle," she said.

"I know."

"There have always been killers in Seattle."

"Yes?"

"Yes," she said and added, "men do not have dreams about longhouses underwater; they have delusions. Wahalachoo could not stop looking for things which never existed. He changed his name for the same reason. But he still could not find anything."

"You don't believe in his vision?"

"Of course I do, but I do not believe in pursuing them. You are either provided with gifts or not; there's no chasing; you have no right to catch what is not yours. It is destructive."

"You mean he kept chasing the longhouse?"

She looked at me again, opening her eyes a bit wider so I could see the orange from the stove set inside them.

"He did what he thought was right. He wanted to find something to make him feel better about all that made him feel wrong. Men here feel wrong and somehow they think owning something is the cure."

"What is the longhouse?" I asked.

"I don't know?" she said. "Perhaps, not worrying. Not dying."

"And, where is it?"

"Nowhere!" she chuckled and shook her head, "You need to listen more."

I apologized.

"Your shirt will take some time. I have things to do before I go into town. Come back for your shirt later. If you even want it?"

"I just want to know," I asked, "when you said all men here feel wrong, you mean the Indian men?"

She focused like she sympathized with my worry and wished she never said anything.

"There's enough to share," she said.

It was easy to unwrap her meaning.

"How much can I give you for the shirt?" I asked.

"Trade when it's ready."

I stood up and walked to the door, but she remained laying down on her bed.

"There was a fire on the water last night," she said.

"What was it? Some sort of vision?"

"No, stupid, it was a boat."

"How big?" I asked.

"Big."

"That's odd."

"Fires happen."

I'll let myself out," I said.

"Close the door, killer."

Xfii

McGilvra's office was the coldest in the firm. On the shelves behind his desk rested heavy streaks of law volumes and between them old relics purchased during his travels around America. Upon his mighty desk stood a stuffed bald eagle encircled by an Indian turtle rattle and a cedar cigar box. The one thing missing from the collection of curiosities was McGilvra himself.

He came out west after appointed US Attorney to the Territory of Washington by President Abraham Lincoln. He travelled extensively, as far east as Idaho, in the territory to keep tabs on court proceedings and settle legal issues to do with large businesses new to the territory. Lawyers in the firm say he was the type of prosecutor who tied a noose around the defendant's neck by the end of the first day of court. To say McGilvra was smart was lazy; he was calculated, tireless, and well connected. He settled down in Seattle years ago and started his firm with Mr. Blain and DeVries, but he ran things how he saw fit and with little resistance. He demanded control.

I stared into the shiny leather backrest of his desk chair and felt like a child dangling his legs inside the rim of a volcano. At any moment McGilvra would open his office door and the caldera would blow.

The mountain popped and the distinguished bearded man who I'd yet to meet stepped to his desk. I stood up to greet him and the two of us faced each other with our chests out and our chins up. He was an American novelty.

"Good day, Mr. Campbell," his iron voice boomed.

"Good day, Mr. McGilvra. It's an honor. Thank—"

"If it's such an honor then why have you been mucking about in my absence, making myself and my firm look like a haven for killers and liars?" he said.

"My apologies, Mr. McGilvra. It was never my intention to bring negativity down upon your firm."

"You didn't for one second think consorting with this Indian killer might look poorly upon your employer?"

"Sir, through circumstances initially beyond my control, I was a witness to the murder of Ms. James."

"The prostitute?"

"Aye, sir."

"Yes?"

"Right, and then Butterfield asked me—as a witness—to look at the second crime scene of Mr. Adams."

"The fornicator."

"Aye, and a drunk, apparently," I said.

"Then what?"

"The killer began to write me."

"And what did you do with these letters?"

"I read them."

McGilvra folded his hands together and rested them on top of his stomach.

"Don't be smart with me Mr. Campbell. Did you turn over the letters to Chief Butterfield?"

"No."

"You should be arrested for withholding evidence."

"I told Butterfield about the letters' contents. The killer rambles on about philosophy and history, Indian stories and how much alike we are. He's crazy."

"Did Butterfield ask for the letters?"

"No, that's why I kept them."

"That's preposterous!"

"Butterfield always was satisfied when I told him the gist of the letters' content."

"Nonetheless, if you are to continue your work here the first thing you are to do is take the letters to the police."

"Aye."

"Were you sent a letter this morning?"

McGilvra's question echoed in my ears, and my conversation with Burke and Furth was still fresh in my mind — there's something odd to do with the latest letter, but I didn't know what, yet.

"It was like the rest."

"It's imperative this letter makes it to Butterfield as well," he said, his voice softening.

"Of course, sir. I'll do it," I said.

"Secondly, I want to know what exactly happened last night."

He took his seat and pulled a thin cigar from the cigar box, tapped the butt-end twice against the armrest of his seat before he cut it and lit it with a crystal table lighter.

"Sit down and talk," he said, exhaling smoke.

"I went to the Hanson Saloon and was attacked from behind by three men who didn't care much for my accent. Before I lost consciousness, I heard the lanterns on the bar break, and screams. I came to in Robert's tent. He said a man he thought was dangerous forced him to take me. He said he wore plain clothes, but police boots. Robert offered to walk me home because I couldn't walk and that's when Butterfield arrested us."

"And then you went home?"

"Yes."

McGilvra stood up and walked to the window from his desk and peeled the curtains back allowing light to splash against his pant legs.

"How long do you think you were unconscious?" he asked.

"I don't know."

"Long enough for the Indian to leave you alone and kill Mr. Bartholomew Richards outside of Yesler's Wharf?"

"I just don't think—"

"You obviously don't know much about thinking or you wouldn't be in this mess," he said.

"Yes, he may have," my blood was starting to warm, "but I don't believe Robert did it."

He walked behind me. Expended cigar smoke seeped from

McGilvra's nostrils. I expected him to touch me, but the smoke disappeared and I could only feel his presence.

"You haven't been here long enough to understand an Indian," he said.

"They're about as trustworthy as one of our Highlanders. My great grandparents were born in Scotland and I grew up hearing the same stories as you. Tales about the English taking our country's sword and scepter, Rob Roy McGregor and the caterans, the 15'and the 45'. They're fun to dream about—the Highlanders—but it's all senseless nostalgia," he smiled. "They were rotten criminals who would stab anyone in the back for a piece of bread. Our Indians are no different. I've seen them cheat and lie in Illinois just the same as in Washington. It isn't their fault being primitive people; but primitives are from a time passed. They honor a different code, one which we refuse to honor any longer."[lxv]

"Robert could read and write. He was educated and didn't have the disposition of a killer."

"And how many have you met, Enoch?"

"I don't see how that's relevant?"

"He was literate—he could have written the letters."

"No."

"Why, no?"

"Before the killer chopped off my hand, he spoke to me about Scotland. Robert thought Scotland was England; it doesn't connect."

"That's tenuous. An Indian knows more about the white man's world then he'll let on."

"He grew up in the white man's world up in Canada," I said, raising my voice. "He couldn't even speak his own language. He was educated by priests in British Columbia."

"You've heard the stories about those priests I'm sure," he said. "Sounds like motive for revenge."

"So, I'm to believe an Indian is a barbarian if he stays an Indian, but if he's educated like a white man then he goes mad?"

"You can't teach out how you're born. Taking away an Indian man's culture is like cutting out his soul. He's going to reclaim his honor somehow; murder is his personal justice. His revenge."

"Then why not kill me? He shouldn't discriminate if he has a vendetta against all whites. It doesn't make sense. That's not it."

"It's in your best interest to start agreeing with me because if it wasn't the Indian running around town killing innocent people then you're next in line."

"Under the false assumption it was either him or I."

McGilvra made his way back to his desk and sat down. He held his cigar up near his eyes and inspected its wrapping with a slight grin.

"You're not quite getting it, are you?"

"I understand people are scared and want the killer to be caught."

"Well then, what's the problem?"

I realized I exercised my maximum amount of freedom of thought. McGilvra's tone was rough and I knew from our short interaction he'd have no issue burying me.

"No problem at all, Mr. McGilvra. I suppose I'd become too comfortable in my role as a witness. Only, I received a letter from the killer this morning, meaning Robert was already arrested and couldn't have sent me—"

"Like I said, those letters are evidence and should immediately be handed over to Butterfield."

"I'll collect them now and drop them to him."

There came a knock at the door.

"Yes?" McGilvra called.

Charles opened the door and poked his head through.

"It's Mr. Colman, sir."

McGilvra looked at me and then back to the door.

"Have him in at once."

McGilvra stood up from his seat and walked towards the door as Colman entered. I stood and turned to greet Mr. Colman, not sure how he would receive me. I noticed Charles back away from the door but keep it ajar to watch Colman and McGilvra shake hands. He watched their exchange closely. His attention then shifted to me. He lifted his eyes to mine and his mouth went flat. He closed the door.

McGilvra looked over to the door and thanked Charles through it. Colman took the opportunity to give me a crushing glare, a look I've only ever witnessed before within the eyes of the Church of Scotland's most staunch supporters. In other words, he was not the least bit happy with me.

I lowered my eyes, but kept them affixed to Colman's to not succumb to cowardice. When my honor felt satisfied, but not overinflated, I removed my eyes and repositioned a chair for him to sit. He stepped forward and took my hand. McGilvra watched us as we shook, and lowered himself into his chair as our embrace concretized.

"I'm writing that letter, Enoch," Colman said.

"I'm at your mercy," I said.

I loosened my grip, but he tightened his.

"I want you to imagine the time it will take to travel there and think very carefully until then of every decision you make."

"I understand, sir."

"It's my hope you do."

He released me from his grip and I felt as though I lost something. McGilvra cut straight into business.

"Jim, how do you feel about Enoch continuing here? I'm quite hurt with the situation he's put this firm into."

"John, I know Enoch's a good lad. I can't tell you what to do with him because I'm the one who asked you the favor of taking him into your service. I feel embarrassed enough things have come to this."

"Is his father as respectable as you say he is?" McGilvra asked.

"Of the finest quality," Colman said.

He looked at me sternly as he said so.

"Then son," McGilvra said, shifting his attention onto me, "you have the honor of four men upon your shoulders right now; your father's, Mr. Colman's, my own, and yourself. I hope you understand the depth and seriousness of what that means here and the penalties for jeopardizing our honor."

"I'm aware, sir and I do not intend to risk the standing of any of your names or the name of my own family in Scotland. The Campbells are in America to do you service and to lay claim to our own enterprise in the Northwest."

"We are aware of the nature of your trip and we welcome you,"

McGilvra said. "I want you to leave my offices and immediately deliver those letters to Butterfield. Once you have done that, return and Charles will introduce you to a large project we are pressed to finish as soon as possible."

"Thank you, sir. I will be at your full disposal."

"Indeed, you will," McGilvra said.

"Enoch, if you could come by our house after your office duties this evening, I would like to have another word with you," Colman said.

"Yes, sir. I can call around as soon as I'm finished here."

"You may leave," McGilvra said.

I walked straight to the door, opened it and left with the feeling I was in both a moral quandary and in immediate and desperate peril. The killer's letters were destined to either save or end me, to which end, I still didn't know.

Xkiii

I returned to Lou's and Anna was still ensnared in her romance novel. She looked up from the book.

"Not needed at the firm today?" she asked, flatly.

"I forgot something in my room."

I went up to the stairs to find my door ajar. I reached for the doorknob when a man opened it and crashed into me, sending me flying.

"A man," was all I could say from the carpet.

I rolled over and watched the long figure drop down the stairs and out of sight. The next I heard a commotion and a thud. The brothel's glass door slammed shut and then shattered. I pulled myself up and ran down the stairs to find an end table overturned and Anna sprawled out on the floor. The doors upstairs began to open and the women congregated. Lou rushed into the room with a perplexed expression.

"What did you do?" she said to me.

I pushed by Lou to Anna, thinking she was stabbed. I knelt beside her and saw swelling and blood around her eye and behind her ear.

"He hit me."

"Who hit you?" Lou said.

"I don't know."

Lou stared at me and shrugged her shoulders as if unconvinced of my innocence.

"He struck my face and I fell over the table and hit my head."

I looked past her and guessed the bureau.

"She's not okay, Enoch," Lou said.

"Anna, what do you remember about him?"

"A black coat." She was struggling. "A hat and a kerchief around his mouth."

"Anything else?"

"Let her be," Lou said. She waved on a few of the lasses from upstairs to help.

"Anna, anything else?" I repeated.

"A bundle of letters."

The women approached and Lou led me away. She pinned me against the wall and was about to give me an earful when Anna's last word connected. I broke free. Lou followed me through the group of lasses and up the stairs. My room was destroyed. The bed ripped open, the drawers emptied and spilled, and the floorboard at the foot of the fireplace pried up.

"They're gone."

"Enoch, what's going on?"

Lou was trembling, and I never thought such a strong woman as she could be frightened. Like me, she was afraid. I stood near her.

"From now on you know nothing about anything," I said. "I don't know what's going on, but we're vulnerable right now."

"I told Furth about the letter this morning," she said.

"I know."

"Jacob and Burke spoke with me."

"They're just trying to help, Enoch."

"That might be so, but right now, I can't trust anyone.

"Jacob's my friend," she said.

"I thought you said there are no friends here?"

"Let's check on Anna—"

"Are you hearing me?" I said.

Lou walked away and down the hall.

"I heard you," she hollered.

Anna was seated on the sofa with two of the older women cleaning the gash above her eye.

"Are you alright?" I asked.

"In shock," she said.

"Anyone would be," her nurse said, blotting the blood from her wound.

"Jess, please pass me my book," Anna asked the other woman attending to her.

"*The Heart of Midlothian*."[lxvi] I said, inspecting the cover.

"Here." She pulled the open envelope from the book and passed it to me.

I looked around and Lou was out of sight. My name was written on its face.

"I'm sorry, Enoch. A man set it on the porch. At the time, I was too upset with you to deliver it."

"What did he look like?" I asked.

"I can't place him, but he was familiar."

"Okay. I'll be back later. But keep this between us."

She nodded.

Lou returned from her office and sat next to Anna. I folded the envelope and discreetly slipped it into my pocket.

"Anna, are you okay?" Lou's eyes were red.

"I must be off," I said, and left knowing I needed do something to make this stop.

Xχiv

I opened the letter. It was type written on sheer typewriter paper.

"June 5th, 1889
"Dear Enoch,

"This letter must be short. I hope you were pleased with my work last night. It's time for us to meet; I have some information about the City Council which will interest you. Meet me above the cabinet shop on Front Street and Madison at 2 o'clock.

— (unsigned)"

I replaced the letter into my coat pocket, satisfied the killer wasn't the author.

"Enoch," Furth greeted me inside the law office, "my apologies for earlier."

Furth extended his hand and smiled. I grasped it and smiled too — if I didn't know whom I could trust I'd have to play my cards closely.

"It's quite alright, Jacob. I think the killings have made us all a bit suspicious."

"Indeed, Enoch," he said and gave my hand a squeeze before releasing it.

"You spoke with John after our conversation?"

"John?"

"McGilvra."

"Oh, yes indeed we did," I said.

"A fruitful mission to San Francisco."

"Beg your pardon?" I asked.

"McGilvra was there on business. We had a representative from the Northern Pacific in town yesterday. Hadn't he mentioned it?"

"No," I said.

"Oh. I'm sorry. I was told Mr. Colman was part of your meeting so I figured it was the topic of discussion. Apologies for assuming."

"None taken," I said. I felt like Furth was dropping me a clue.

"And did you turn the letters into Butterfield?"

"No, Jacob. Someone beat me to it and ran out of Lou's with them, injuring one of her lasses on the way out."

The news cleaned the smile from his face. I then walked past him and into McGilvra's office. Burke and Yesler were there.

"Excuse you, young man," McGilvra boomed.

"The letters were stolen from my room," I said.

Yesler and Burke stood from their chairs.

"They were what?" Burke said.

"An assailant knocked me over and dashed out with them."

"Charles!" McGilvra yelled.

Charles entered the office behind me.

"Yes, Mr. McGilvra," he said, looking flushed.

"Notify Butterfield the letters were stolen from Mr. Campbell's bedroom."

"Sir?" he said in a worried tone.

"Charles, leave now."

"Yes, sir." He paused, then spoke, "Have we forgotten to consider Mr. Campbell is perhaps responsible?"

"There are witnesses," I said, surprised with the allegation.

"Charles?" McGilvra replied in surprise of his assistant's audacity.

"Witnesses do not account for an accomplice," Charles replied.

"My accomplice is in jail, is he not?" I said.

"Don't be coy," Yesler hammered.

"Charles, we are more than equipped with the power of deduction," McGilvra said, "Now go."

Charles withdrew from the office. I saw him out and noticed the cuffs of his trousers were rimmed in mud.

"Enoch," McGilvra said, "do you have any idea who stole them?"

I turned back to McGilvra.

"Only the lass, Anna, saw him. She said he was swathed in black."

"They're always in black," Yesler snickered, "In the daylight, why don't they wear white?"

"It's too muddy to wear white," I said.

Yesler's mouth clamped down, and he stared at me.

"Was his latest letter one of the stolen?" McGilvra asked.

"Yes," I said, withholding the fact there were two.

Burke exhaled a deep breath, as if relieved.

"And what did he say?" Yesler asked.

I looked at McGilvra.

"Go on, boy," he said.

"He wants to meet."

"Will you?"

"Of course not," I said.

"Mention nothing of this final letter, Enoch. It's imperative," McGilvra said.

"I don't understand," I said.

"Not until we unravel this."

"Yes, sir."

"Now back to your work and nothing more."

McGilvra walked me to the door and shut it. There was plenty to discuss with me on the outside.

Xxv

I smelled the roast from a block away. It mixed well with the scent of the salty bay and cedar smoke from the encampments below. Colman's home was the brightest on the block—gas-lit. The mixing scents reminded me of the summers when my father and I would take leave of Glasgow for my uncle's house on the Isle of Skye. The trip frightened me, for the Minch[lxvii] was always rough and made me seasick. However, when we arrived there was always a roasted leg of lamb waiting for us—and it made the trip worth the waves.

My uncle was mad, as mad as my mother, but in his own way. His house was our family castle; purchased by my grandfather after he visited the Isle and fell in love with the way of life there, a life he persisted was the real way of our Scottish ancestors. My uncle's excitement to inhabit a moss-eaten and decrepit home was justified through the same romantic idealization. Though everyone took a jab or two at my uncle for nursing his need for authenticity at the expense of the family bank, his time in India with the 1st Bengal-Fusiliers left him shattered enough that no one in the family had the gall to question his motives. My father's opinion on the matter was his brother deserved his repose upon the shores of the dark sea due to the ominous twists of fate which plagued the experiences of his youth.

My uncle often took me on long walks when my father was locked in his bedchambers drafting letters, and spoke to me at length about the Indian Rebellion. Though there only seemed to me generalities in common between India's Union with England to that of Scotland's one hundred and fifty years before, it was close enough a comparison for my uncle. He would go on about how England wanted the whole world to become 'pock-puddings' and answer to Westminster; to read only Shakespeare and Milton and be smug about it to the illiterate who kept their engines stocked with coal. He was a hurt man.

I cared little for his tirades as I saw nothing that could be done to change the matter. However, on other occasions, when he was in a less agitated spirit of mind, he'd recount the strangeness of India. He'd tell stories about man-eating tigers and of the hunters made famous by tracking them deep into the jungle and slaying them. He told me of thin men in loincloths who would stuff themselves inside small trunks and stay knotted up in them for days at a time without food or water.

I remember one particularly gruesome story. It was somewhere outside of Delhi during the hot season, and his company arrived into a large village just before sunset. The village, said my uncle, was diseased with the psychological blackness of futility, as it became obvious days before the rebellion was crushed. Upon arrival, there stood several large trees with slithering arms, and hanging off those arms, black from blocking the light emanating from the sunset behind, the stretched bodies of seven women. He mentioned the queerest aspect of the horrific sight came when he walked to the other side of the tree, where the sunset was at his back. There, the women were no longer in the shadows and their garments glowed like rubies and sapphires. They looked as though they should be set on fire.

I cannot forget how methodically he recounted the story, and his explanation of his reaction when he stood under them. He said he'd seen so much death and rape in India the hanging women triggered evil in him because he didn't feel sorry for them. Instead of sadness, he felt the impulse to set their corpses on fire and destroy them, their image, and his memory.

Once I heard this story, and the myriad of associations he made between the suicides of India and the self-immolation of Highland women during the Highland clearances, the mass murdering of seafowl we conducted together by rifle became far scarier to me because of the pleasure he seemed to take from it. I was never sure during the frenzy of shots and falling birds if he would turn the gun on me. I thought of evil as an infection, one you cannot be cured of once exposed. I supposed him killing me would have been out of some sick sense of love, and the plausibility of my end coming by way of my uncle's madness in turn made Glasgow's own insanity somehow less worrisome. The city was a better alternative to the unpredictable nature of my uncle's woeful nostalgia, and I preferred the smoke to the sea air. I preferred my father's brick Bessy to my Uncle's gothic prison.

However, this is all superfluous information to the main fact, in those days when I was a boy on the Isle of Skye, I found our evening roasts of mutton and nips of malt the sole source of warmth in my uncle's castle.

·   ·   ·   ·   ·

I stepped to the door to knock, but it swung open before my knuckles could connect.

"Evening, Enoch."

"Evening, James."

"Well, come in lad, the house will catch cold," he said, trying to smile.

I entered the foyer and the perfume of roasting lamb filled my nostrils.

"Lamb," I said, looking back to him in surprise, "How on earth did you find lamb?"

"An old friend from San Francisco was up this way and kept it on ice the entire sail up."

"An old business partner?"

"A railroad man with the Northern Pacific."

"Not the most liked entity here, I've heard."

"Aye, but still a necessary one," he said.

"Are you still laying track?"

"These mitts are in many pots, Enoch," he said, raising his open palms. "Come inside our castle."

He showed me into his living room.

The pine ceiling loomed exposed and unstained with a stark simplicity which contrasted the ornate wallpaper. The room was sparse; nothing existed there which wasn't necessary. The sofas appeared unused, the end tables held boring lamps, and the rugs looked combed and tiptoed around. Colman stood staring from the foyer, proud to watch me catalogue his possessions—or perhaps paranoid I might touch them. On an adjacent mantle sat a tattered sporran[lxviii] and a dingy bonnet.

"Still Scottish, I see."

He walked over to the old relics.

"They have been in the family for a generation. They belonged to my grandfather—made for George IV's visit to Scotland."

"I take it these lamps are from the continent?" I asked.

"The lamps and the rugs are French. The sofas were made in Germany but purchased in London."

"Very tasteful."

"I will retrieve Agnes, she's busy putting the final touches on tea."

Colman left the room.

I looked again at Colman's sporran and the walls of my uncle's castle returned to my thoughts. History bled from the masonry, but nothing bleeds from Colman's new house, just as the modern buildings in Seattle contain no soul. Still, Colman's home dominates what surrounds it—and just how my family's castle towered over the sea, Colman's towers over Angeline's cabin on the beach below it. It's troubling to think this structure could stand for the next hundred years, but through a moderate storm, Angeline's could be gone by morning. I wondered what Colman's house would look like in a hundred years after everyone who saw it new, was dead. The next generation will think this empty home is haunted. They'll perhaps think this house was built when structures meant something. They will invent a meaning for it. Nostalgia isn't a memory, but a filler.

Regardless of the future, the newness of the house lent little to feeling at home within it, and Colman's Scottish relics lost their meaning being placed on a clean surface. It's only the roast that evoked feelings for Scotland, but that as well was hollow. It would take too much creativity and self-deception to believe Scotland exists within a meal, or even in a castle.

Colman's butler entered. The strange concierge and barkeep from the Brunswick Hotel, the night of the chase. He was gangly and opaque. He smiled at me and his teeth appeared held together with mortar. He pointed to the door he came from.

"The dining room."

It must be him.

"Have we not met?" I asked.

"I'm sorry, but I have no recollection," he responded, still with a smile on his face.

"Do you work in the Brunswick?"

"The hotel?" His smile slipped away as Colman interrupted from the other room.

"Enoch, come to the dining room," he said.

I left the strange man and entered the large room where the Colmans were seated at the far end of a long table.

"Your setting is here, son," Agnes said.

I could feel the butler standing close behind me, and I turned around to find his chin hanging over my head.

"Please, sir," he said, motioning to the table.

I sat.

"It's good to see you, Enoch," Agnes said.

"Yes, indeed it is. Twice in a day," Colman added.

"How is your hand?" she asked.

"It's better, but often I think I can still feel it, and it aches."

"How awful and strange."

Both Colmans shifted in their seats—I had already made things awkward.

"We heard about what happened at Lou's today," Colman said, changing the subject.

"Yes, the letters," I said.

"How on earth did the killer know the letters were hidden under a slat of wood next to the fireplace?" Agnes asked. "And how were you in possession of police evidence?"

"Have you spoken with Lou?" I asked, confounded by her knowledge of the incident.

"Jacob Furth told us."

"Of course," I said to Colman. "He was in the office after you left."

"It's an odd coincidence the theft happened just after our discussion with McGilvra."

"Aye, very," I said without sounding disingenuous.

"And are you hurt?"

"No."

There was a moment of silence while we ate.

"I hear the killer wants to meet you," Colman said.

"You better do no such thing," Agnes said.

"Not planning to."

Colman cleared his throat.

"The lamb is good," I said.

"Yes, not as good as fresh, but good," Agnes said. "It must make you think of home?"

"Yes, it does."

"I canna fathom home sometimes; it's been so long since we flitted off to America," she said. "I miss so many things."

"As do I," I said.

They both resituated their bodies as if whatever I said made them uncomfortable.

"I'm sorry," Agnes said.

"There's no need, Mrs. Colman; I too miss the humor and the hills."

She relaxed.

"And you will be returning?" she said.

Colman shot her a look, but she kept her eyes pinned to mine.

"I'm not aware I am."

"With this business of the killer and that idiot Butterfield, you're best to flee, boy," she said.

"Agnes," Colman said.

"James," she fired back, "the boy's in danger."

"Aye, and I have told him I plan to write his father about the business of the murder."

"And does the post fly faster than the killer's inspiration?" she said.

"The killer, as far as we know, has been apprehended."

"That young Indian man killing children with a hammer? I think not, James."

Colman raised his voice.

"Enough!"

I dropped my fork on the plate, picked it up, and continued to struggle with my lamb.

The table fell silent.

"Dear, let me cut your meat for you," Agnes said.

"I couldn't possibly have you—"

She was already up and stood beside me to cut up the slab of lamb on my plate. Colman turned away to spare me the embarrassment. Agnes returned to her chair.

The butler shook his head and laughed. Colman cleared his throat.

"McGilvra told me you will work with Charles on Furth's water works plan. That should be a good bulk of work to keep you busy until I hear back from your father."

"Yes, I reviewed the maps today," I said. "It's a mess, isn't it?"

"And now this bloody flush toilet makes things even messier."

"Aye, when the tide's in to be sure."

"This is not a conversation for the table, gentleman," Agnes said.

James and I shared a smile.[lxix]

"Yes, but the issue is a complex one," he said.

"I don't see how we can replace an entire network."

"That's the challenge, isn't it?"

"I must admit, another situation which feels insurmountable."

"Confusing times, Enoch," Colman said.

"It's hard to concentrate with half the city thinking I'm in some way involved with the killings."

"All will come out right, just as long as you keep away from trouble."

"Yes, but I feel as though I'm a hair away from arrest. I've done nothing wrong."

"As I said, withdraw yourself and keep busy."

Colman looked at me gravely and then smiled.

"I suppose it's the smartest road to take," I said.

I peered at Colman, and he cocked his head, still smiling.

"Lad, I suggest you begin doing what you were sent here to do."

"I will."

"And then, you can leave," Colman said.

We were now engaged in a silent dialogue.

Agnes looked at her plate, pulled her serviette from her lap, and dabbed the corners of her mouth.

"We're practically family, and as fellow countrymen, I hope we're not beginning a standoff during supper," she said.

Colman stood from his seat, approached me, and gripped my shoulder. He kept on his false smile and nodded to his wife.

"No, my dear, I'm just worried and feel he needed a stern talking to."

"And maybe I have, James," I said to also relieve the tension.

He returned to his seat and stared—indeed still intent to continue our silent dialogue.

"The boy has learned his lesson," Agnes said to Colman. "I'm sure along with his hand, his sense of foolish adventure was also removed."

"Aye, the romance died in that moment, and the full force of my situation came bearing down when the killer pinned me to the street with his foot."

"An extreme scenario we wish no loved one to experience," Colman interjected. "But yes, every young man must have his moment where the real world supplants the romantic."

"I see that now."

I'd never seen Colman as a menacing man, but at the dinner table it was obvious that I'd been warned.

•　　•　　•　　•　　•

Supper was finished and the mysterious butler, who I swore I recognized from before, entered the dining room again.

"The escort has arrived," he said, smiling.

Colman paid no mind to him and continued to smoke.

"Your escort home should be here any minute," he said.

I turned to look at the butler who had returned to his position behind me, but he wasn't there.

"Escort?" I said, confused.

"Yes, to take you home."

"I prefer to walk."

"Where has your preferences taken you so far?"

"Into trouble," Agnes answered.

"I imagine I have little choice in the matter?"

"Indeed, we insist."

"But, isn't the killer caught?" I asked.

"It's more to do with your protection from those who think you might be involved."

The young officer Foley, who escorted me home the night before, entered the dining room with his hat fit snug between his forearm and hip. Tonight, he was in uniform.

"You?" he said.

I looked at the Colmans.

"I take your meaning on the matter."

•   •   •   •   •

I was shown out of the house into the night and the smell of roasted hogget was replaced with horse manure, which stirred the memory of my encounter with the killer inside the Langston Livery.

"Odd I'm taking you home again," he said after a minute of us rolling down the hill towards Lou's.

"It has been a day of oddity," I said.

Foley appeared confused.

"I don't understand, sir."

"It doesn't matter."

We were quiet again.

"I know you didn't do it," Foley said.

"Aye?" I said. "Why?"

"Because the Indian did it."

"And how do you know that?"

"He admitted it."

"bollocks," I said.

"We made it so," he said.

Dublin, 1916

He killed him. His hatred of hospitals, smugness, and his need to cure his hangover killed Cormac. Dooley was drinking on Camden Street, at a public house with no public. He sat alone, wallowing. Thinking. Thinking hard about Cormac and about Enoch. Enoch the handless. Enoch the hunted. The killer. The manuscript had gone mad, but it was working on the doctor. Dooley questioned Enoch's guilt now, when before he was sure. Enoch was changing. Even though the multitude of letters in the manuscript was nonsense; Enoch's conversations in perfect English with an Indian woman, improbable; and the implication a city's whole council was complicit in a mass conspiracy, completely reckless. However, Enoch's narrative read as too strange to be fiction.

Dooley felt if only he could find someone in Dublin who lived in Seattle at that time then maybe he could unbolt himself from Enoch's story to gain clarity on the situation. There must to be someone. But, there didn't. It would be rare; who would come back to Ireland?

Seated alone, Dooley muttered an indecipherable tapestry of expletives and the pub manager came to check on him.

"You alright?" he asked.

"Grand, grand," Dooley said.

"Says yourself."

"A good man has died."

"Oh, right. Sorry."

"Sorry?" Dooley said.

The manager knew not to respond.

"I'm the sorry one here."

He poured the doctor another pint beside his better judgment.

Dooley winced at the pub manager as a form of thank you, which translated into a pitiful request for an open ear.

"You see," Dooley said, "I've this patient, aye a patient who told me a tale, and the story is an ook one. He gave me an excuse for not coming to his appointment and—"

"Sorry doctor, but what are ye on about?" the pub manager said.

Dooley stopped and rolled his eyes up to the ceiling and thought for a second.

"I don't know?" he said, dropping his gaze back to the pub manager.

"I thought ye were on about yer man dying, not some patient?"

"Aye, they're connected, but never you mind."

"Now you've got me interested. How're they connected?" The pub manager asked.

"At best, the patient kens who killed my friend, and at worst, he did the deed himself."

"This the journalist who was mugged last night?"

"It was no mugging," Dooley said.

"But ye know who did it?"

"I wouldn't go that far, man," Dooley said, "but I would say I've myself mixed up in something bad."

"You've thought about the RIC haven't ye?"

"I've no proof."

"In fairness, they've never needed proof before."

"The problem I'm having is—oh, it's impossible to explain," Dooley said.

"Go on."

Dooley hesitated and recounted Enoch's digressive juxtaposition between his uncle's castle on the Isle of Skye and Colman's empty house. He thought of the oddity of a bonnet and sporran sitting in an empty house and then of Enoch's unclear tragedy. The butler. Dooley was missing something important.

"I should remember him," Dooley said.

"Well, he's your patient, isn't he? I would hope so."

"Don't be daft," Dooley said.

A confused look overtook the barkeep and he shook his head.

"Doctor, maybe you should head back to your office and take a nap? With your man's killing, maybe you need a good cup of tea and a rest."

"No tea, my maid's gone," Dooley said, staring blankly across the bar, lost in his thoughts.

The barkeep came across the bar and helped the doctor off his stool.

"No charge, doctor, but please get yourself somewhere to sleep it off."

"Aye, I'll come back later and pay."

"No bother, no bother at all doctor."

Dooley stumbled out of the pub and was relieved the day reached dusk. He crossed Camden Street and went through an alleyway toward Harcourt Street. Behind him were two men. Both appeared respectable enough but quickly gained on him. He imagined Cormac lying dead in his coach covered with blood. The thought made him nervous and the men, menacing. He scuttled through the bottleneck of the alley onto Harcourt, hoping to reach the main drag before the men caught up to him. The two men dodged a few other passersby and overtook Dooley with no malice. The doctor cowered. They turned around to face him and laughed. Dooley felt the worse for it and didn't mind his step off the footpath. He stumbled into the street and in front of an oncoming trolley. He froze, but a strong hand grasped his collar and yanked him out of the street and back onto the footpath.

"Never mind the killer is onto you," the stranger whispered into his ear, "you're doing well enough endangering your life walking around full of piss."

The Glaswegian's hand set the swimming doctor down on the footpath like a kettle, and all Dooley could see of him were two opaque figures in long coats focus into one as the man hurried away.

"Hey, yoo come back here," he said to the apparition. "Sod yoo, Enoch. Come back here and help an aging fool off the footpath."

Glaring at the doctor in a fit of awe, his two false assailants snapped out of their paralysis and came to Dooley's aid. They picked him up by his coat arms, and Dooley swatted their hands away and gave chase for the Glaswegian, jogging in a zigzag pattern, which restored their laughter at the old fool.

●　　●　　●　　●　　●

Caught in the octopus's knot off Grafton Street—off Wicklow Street, below Clarendon where William Street meets the head of Church Lane—a body hung from the tower of the ancient church there. It swayed in the evening breeze above the glowing amber street lanterns. The dead man's ankles were tied. Head cracked half off. Red raindrops patterned the stone footpath beneath. The girl standing below him in a wool dress danced in place like she was drunk or half asleep. She fell into a heap and began to convulse. The sight caused a horrific panic, and Dooley ran right into it.

"Is there a doctor?" a woman shouted.

Dooley pushed through the small crowd and saw the girl shaking on the ground. Two men pinned her shoulders.

"Release her!"

The two men looked up at Dooley with overloaded eyes, and the younger looking of the two stood up.

"I'm glad she's doing what she's doing, or I'd be looking up at something much worse," he said.

"Help me roll her," Dooley said.

"What?"

"I'll give you a hand," Enoch said, crouched over the girl.

Dooley froze and the horrific situation before him ceased to matter in the second it took for him to recognize the middle-aged man before him from a time long ago. He watched Enoch monitor the girl's spasms. Enoch showed no sign of worry or fear. Dooley thought him first a doctor by his cool head, but the stranger appeared to have no medical training. His composure despite the situation led Dooley to believe Enoch experienced much worse in his life; perhaps the macabre events depicted in his story. A witness or killer was still to be decided.

Dooley's own experience with death taught him a great deal about how people stomach the distress of witnessing the end of another's life. To the doctor, Enoch acted clinically. His eyes were inhabited with the look of urgency, not lust. Dooley knew the lustful gaze affixed to the faces of affluent heirs and heiresses watching their benefactors fade away. He imagined a killer would look upon his work the same.

"Don't resist her movements," the doctor said to Enoch, "but keep her from hurting herself any further."

The doctor rolled up her long and laced sleeve, and the inside of her elbow joint was smudged with coagulated blood.

"What do you make of this, Enoch?" Dooley said.

They locked eyes and the doctor's chamber door of old forgotten memories stirred.

"You and I both know this is a message," Enoch said.

"The little girl in Seattle?"

"Aye, and what's worse he's not sending letters, but bodies."

"Cormac," Dooley said.

"I've work to do doctor, but know you're in danger."

"Wait a minute, now," Dooley said. "You can't leave me here."

"You need to finish the book first," Enoch said.

He then left and melded into the crowd of onlookers. The church bell began to toll and the onlookers looked up to the hanging man.

All was quiet and still on the little bend off Grafton Street.

Xxvi

This time I didn't need to talk officer Foley out of tucking me into bed. He dropped me in front of Lou's and set off for the police station's livery without looking back. I approached Lou's and heard a busy night emanate from the building's broken door. I entered and squeezed through the fudge of shoulders and stares until I got to the steps.

"Enoch."

I turned around.

"Lou."

"Well?" She questioned with her hands splayed out like she was about to catch something falling from the ceiling. "Who took them?"

"The letters?" I asked.

"What else?"

"I don't know who took them—maybe the killer?"

I didn't have an answer, but I felt a trigger go off in my stomach like I knew the answer, but just hadn't worked it out in my mind yet.

"Enoch?" she asked me, seeing I lost my train of thought. "What's wrong, you look sad?"

Lou, showing emotion, meant she was drunk, which indeed she was.

"I'm fine," I said.

"Anna would like a word with you. She thinks she recognized the man who delivered the letter to the door this morning, and also something about Mr. Richards. But, I'm confused? Were there two letters?"

My hairs stood on end, but I kept my mouth closed and my eyes from growing wide. I warned Anna not to say anything; Lou can't keep her mouth shut. I needed to make sure no one knew about the second letter; everyone had to think I'd only seen the fake one.

"Maybe she can talk you out of meeting that maniac while you're up there?"

Lou knew me well enough to know despite what I'd said to McGilvra, there's no way I'd refuse a meeting with the killer, even with the knowledge it was a set up.

"I just saw one letter, Lou," I said. Where's Anna?"

"In her room, she was not feeling well."

I pushed through the crowd and up the stairs to Anna's room and knocked on the door. There was no answer. I tried the door, it was open. I walked in and saw her lying on top of her bed, the covers sprayed with vomit, her eyes bulging from their sockets.

My ears began to ring and I felt my tie constrict around my throat.

"Enoch," Lou said.

She entered the room and screamed.

"No," she said and ran out.

I couldn't turn away. The feeling in the room was familiar. I failed her.

Two men ran up behind me, into the room and stopped dead in their tracks.

"Jesus Christ," one said.

"What happened to her?"

I couldn't respond.

"What happened?" the one repeated.

"Witnessed a mistake," I said.

Xxvii

They were all dead in their beds. She was asleep. She slept the whole night. I didn't. I sat beside the bed, my head resting on her boney forearm. The stubble of two-day grow-out pushed between the scales of her reptilian skin. It was a slow race—both of us running from the inevitable, running from the truth of it all, and we were tired. Our relay was bound to breakdown. She told me in more ways than one she would be the one to drop the baton. She wanted to drop it, but I didn't. I could keep going. I could run until my grip would shatter the object which kept us united. But she didn't want that. She only ran for me. She knew more than I did about how the race works, how all races have a finish line no matter where you place, but I couldn't see it. And so, when I faded into dreams—delirious, desperate, not able to fight sleep any longer—she finished the race without me.

My head rested on her cooling body. I dreamed of the sea and the high cliffs which cradled my uncle's house below it. When I roused, it was just I. The last runner left. Abandoned. The feeling possessed my breath and forced my lungs out of my mouth. It was an inexplicable feeling. Everything in the inside—my lungs, my vital organs, and my heart—all wanted out. The feeling was emptiness, a vacuum. She was dead and I died too. We were dead together, yet in my hand she left the baton. So, before the nurses and the doctors and our families could notice the conclusion of our race I grabbed a scalpel and ran to continue the fantasy, or at least to find a quiet place to die.

The trees flashed as I ran past them. Deeper and deeper I plunged into the forest outside the sanitarium. The trees' dressing of undergrowth reached out to impede my escape, but they failed to hold me. Nature suggests things, gives gentle advice, but I ignored it. My wife was taken by something natural.

I stopped. Slashed. It ached to feel the blood escape. I lay on the ground and looked up into the leafless spokes of an ancient oak and saw a wheel spin to a stop. I closed my eyes and there stood the sea cliffs and my uncle shooting gulls in the background. My wife was missing. I was the dead man with the baton and no wife. Her name was Flora.

Xℓviii

I sat in McGilvra's office, the room soaked in silence, and stared at the cigar box set between the stuffed eagle and turtle rattle on his desk. He checked his watch and then put it away. He seemed nervous. Butterfield let himself in.

"Can you tell us anything else about the last conversation you had with Anna?" he asked.

"No."

They wanted to know if she mention anything about Richards. Anna's client that was supposed to be lying outside Yesler's Wharf and not in her bed.

"Did she seem worried?"

"She was in shock," I said.

"Did she know the identity of the killer?"

"I don't know. I don't think so."

"We interviewed Lou. She said Anna recognized whoever had dropped off the killer's letter."

"I thought you had the killer in custody? Didn't he confess?"

Butterfield resituated himself in his chair.

"We're looking for the truth," he said.

"Is it true the killer, in his letter, asked for a meeting this afternoon? Lou said the girl mentioned it."

"Aye."

"We want you to go," Butterfield said.

"Why would I do that?"

"To trap him."

I knew this was a trap, but of a different kind than what they were suggesting.

The door opened and an older man with thick spectacles put his head through the opening. No Charles.

"Mr. McGilvra, Mr. Colman is here to see you."

"See him in," McGilvra said.

Butterfield trained his eyes on Colman and refused to consider mine.

"Chief Butterfield would like to use your boy here to catch the killer," McGilvra said.

"Absolutely not," Colman said.

"I agree; it's obvious the killer wants to finish him off."

"Enoch?" Butterfield asked.

"Yes, me?" I said. "What if he's ready to end it with me?"

"I thought you said he's too fond of you for that?" Butterfield replied.

"I'm not sure of anything anymore."

I thought about Robert—I'd catch the killer to clear his name.

"If I catch him what becomes of Robert?"

"If the killer admits to the tavern massacre and the murder of Mr. Richards, he's a free man."

Butterfield's face burned beet red. Colman and McGilvra eyed each other like they were unsure of what was going on.

"It's the sure-fire way to prove your innocence," Butterfield added.

"I'll do it," I said.

"I cannot allow it," Colman interjected.

"The boy's spoken," Yesler said, standing inside the door. "That bastard stole the scantlings from my trees this morning. I want him caught and hung."

The men turned to Yesler.

"It's about Goddamn time that embarrassing scar was wiped off those trees," McGilvra said, before adding, "What the hell are you doing here?"

Burke emerged from behind Yesler.

"Thomas? This was a private meeting, gentleman."

"Sorry to intrude, but Furth is meant to meet me here to go over some legal with Charles," Burke said.

"Mr. Bertrand isn't in," McGilvra replied.

"I see. I'll wait for Furth outside," he said.

Yesler was still at the door.

"And Henry, what do you want?"

"I saw Thomas head this way, and thought I'd come join."

"Well, shut the door behind you, Henry."

Yesler chuckled and walked out leaving the door ajar.

Butterfield went over the plan he devised and it was quite simple. Several plain-clothed police would be handy in the unlikely event the killer decides to murder me, and the rest of the force will hide out in an adjacent building until I lure the killer into the open. It was an awful plan. I was to meet at the police station at two o'clock. I asked if I could have some alone time to prepare myself for the meeting. I pleaded Anna's death was still fresh in my mind. All agreed, besides Butterfield, as I figured.

I digested the queer feeling I was playing into someone else's scheme and my plan was not my own. Perhaps they knew I knew it was a trap? Or, they were using me for a higher end which I was unaware of? I felt as though I had just hours to live. Regardless, I was going to see it through. I couldn't live with myself if I didn't. Those fuckers may not have killed everyone, but they certainly killed Anna.

Dublin, 1916

The girl died, there was too much poison in her veins. Dooley held her and could feel her diaphragm struggle to produce a breath. It wasn't long before her breathing became too shallow to notice. Her skin bleached below her father's hanging body. That was it.

Dooley was home. It was early morning on Good Friday and he hadn't slept a wink. He made cup after cup of tea to finish Enoch's tale. He remembered him now. The doctor recalled how much he hated the boy for his reaction when his wife died; Enoch's performance disrupted the prescribed numbness which was mandatory for Dooley to do his job inside the sanitarium. Enoch's attempt to take his own life slaughtered a lot of hope that day.

However, Dooley didn't have the energy to further investigate the dry entrails of his old and angry memories. Instead, he allowed himself to recall his own moments of calamity, and for once he sympathized with Enoch and felt wretched for holding the worst day in the young man's life against him. Soft with age.

Enoch's life was a strange one. Dooley scanned the scattered pages of his manuscript which were strewn across his bedroom floor. By the end of it, he felt he'd come to understand why ghosts haunt. Enoch's life was a chain of kinks and failed clasping. There were events so extreme in Enoch's life, the vacuous space they must have left within his poor soul would surely suck his spirit back in time upon his death. He feared the man would spend his eternity with his uncle on the Isle of Skye shooting birds until the lid of heaven caved in and all celestial life ceased to be, along with the living. Dooley wished to be wrong. Soft with age.

What Dooley was left with now—in the life of the living—was a caper. A true who-done-it he was unwillingly enrolled and expected to participate in. The doctor considered the killer was at that very moment outside of his flat, looking in his window. He felt the little hairs on his neck stand on end, but it excited him, and strangely he enjoyed the feeling. He knew Enoch enjoyed it too. Enoch's experiences in Seattle changed him—how could they not? He lost his wife, left Scotland, and death followed him to America. Enoch's a conduit for death—Dooley was too, and that's what united them. They were both part of something terrible and invincible. Death needed them to spread its word.

The game changed for the doctor. This go-around, he aimed to save those on death's list, and to do so by hunting death itself. He owed it to Enoch and himself to sever their ties with the killer, once and for all, even if that meant to die himself. Dooley couldn't be sure if he meant for his death to be metaphorical or physical, but he knew he was no longer afraid of death. Something had changed inside of him. The killings shook him awake and to care about people again. He'd waited for the fuse to be lit. His great act, something to excuse his apathy and intemperance while in the presence of God.

The doctor bent down to collect Enoch's manuscript when a flaming bottle smashed through his window, whirled across the room, and shattered against the wall. Blue flame crawled across the wall and coughed a hot wind back at Dooley. He stood up, looked at the fire and felt death was close. He rushed to the window and a man in a grey suit stood looking up at him. He then casually turned and walked away towards the Liffey.

The heat from the fire touched the back of the doctor's neck and roused him. He collected his coat and ran past the fire to the bedroom door, but the door wouldn't budge. He pounded, kicked and scratched at it, but it was solid shut. The flame was growing and spreading to the ceiling. Dooley ran back to the window and began to holler for help. His neighbor opened his window and poked his head out.

"Thom," he said, tired-eyed and half asleep, "what's the matter?"

"Eamon, my room is on fire and my bedroom door's locked shut.

Take my key and get me out of here."

Eamon's eyes opened wide as he saw wisps of smoke escape above Dooley's head and out the window. Dooley dangled his keys in front of him and tossed them across. There was a moment when it appeared Eamon misjudged Dooley's shallow toss, but he was able to stretch out his arm and make the catch.

"Jesus, Thom."

Within moments Dooley heard banging at his front door. Eamon began to holler for others in the building to help him. The fire spiraled across the ceiling and raged out of his window. Inside, the smoke began to build, crawling lower and lower down the walls. He kicked at his bedroom door, but it wouldn't budge. From below he heard pounding and wood breaking. The smoke overwhelmed the desperate doctor and forced him onto the floor.

He heard a loud crack through the floor and then a flurry of footsteps trample up his stairs.

"Thom, where are you?" Eamon yelled.

"In here!"

Dooley heard his neighbors trying to get at the door and after a collective heave-ho a pearl of light returned inside the door's keyhole.

"We're going to kick in the door."

Dooley's room was now too inundated with smoke for him to answer without taking in a breath of the noxious gasses. The door swung open and the men grabbed the doctor, dragging him out into the hallway. Dooley was then led down the stairs. A line of neighbors ran the opposite direction with pails of water to squelch the blaze. Once on the street, Dooley collapsed to his hands and knees and began to cough. When he was finished he wiped the saliva and soot from his face. He thought of whisky. He thought of death. He feared it after all. Pathetic, he thought. I can't hang onto one noble idea. Soft with age.

XƗIƗ

I stepped into the street with a couple hours to figure out how I was going to survive my execution. I hadn't an answer, so I figured I'd pay Angeline for the shirt. I walked up the steep grade to the encampment and was tired when I arrived. She was hanging laundry.

"It's easier to come here by canoe," she said.

"I didn't know."

"You can't paddle anyway."

"No, I can't," I said.

"The stains didn't come out of your shirt."

"They didn't?"

"So, I cut the shirt into rags."

"I'll still pay you for your effort."

"Pay me for rags?" She was confused.

"No, for trying to take out the stains."

"No need."

The air drew out of the conversation and in the quiet, I felt fear. I was afraid of what was to come later.

"I'm supposed to meet the killer later today," I said.

Angeline didn't react and pinned a pair of socks to the line.

"The police say they want me to help catch him, but it's a trap."

She continued working.

"I don't know for sure who's responsible for the killings."

"You don't need to," she responded, "because it's none of your business."

I didn't follow.

"What do you mean?"

"Just that," she said. "Who chases their own death?"

"I do."

"Then, you'll get what you want."

"But I don't want to die."

"Then don't die."

"I'll do my best," I said. "I have to go. It's the only way I can get justice for Anna and Robert."

She didn't answer.

"Angeline, can you tell me more about the fire?"

She dropped her hands from pinning a shawl to the line and took a deep breath.

"It was far away on the water and glowed for a few minutes," she said.

"Anything else?"

"A smaller boat sailed in with a dim lantern."

She finished with her laundry.

"Go away now," she said. I was surprised.

"I'm sorry. I didn't mean to offend?"

"You have no humor," she said.

"How can I right now?"

"How can you not?" she said, and stepped up onto her porch. "Now go." She pointed back to the city.

I walked away.

Her neighbor raised his hand and gave me a slow-wave goodbye. Maybe he was beginning to like me?

XXX

I entered Lou's and she sat at the bar alone with a bottle of bourbon.

"I've agreed to go," I said.

"I know," she answered without removing her gaze from the windows.

"They must be confused," I said.

"About what?"

"You must have told them I received two letters yesterday."

"It was evidence. I told Furth about the letter," she said.

"It was Anna's fault for telling you."

"We all know that maniac is still loose. You misjudged him."

"Believe what you need to," I said.

She took a drink and then poured a glass for me. I stood at the bar.

"They're tying up their loose ends," I said.

"They?"

"The Council," I said. "They killed Anna. She could tie Richards to here when he was supposed to be dead."

"The killer has poisoned your mind," she said.

"I'll tell you what doesn't make sense."

"What's that?" she said.

"The typed letter."

"Yeah?"

"I think it was never supposed to reach me."

"Believe whatever you need to," she responded. "But know, the waters are muddied, and you could be wrong."

We both took a drink. I finished first and slammed it down. Lou jumped.

"I'm sorry I ever trusted you," I said, and walked towards the door.

"I told them to protect you, not to see you dead," she said. "I also have a hotel to run."

"Not for long."

I headed toward the doorway.

"Why do you care anyway?" she said. "It's not as though you've ever shown you give a shit about anyone but yourself."

I stalled and thought about Flora; but her image, still plagued by flies and disease since the day she died, remained obscured. The image of my mother overtook the black mass but subsided. They were replaced by Anna and Robert, holding hands with the girl from the alley. I was to fail.

"I'm trying," I said. "I just don't know how to feel anymore."

She dropped her guard and bowed her head.

"Be careful Enoch; there's a killer out there and it's not the Council."

I walked out the door knowing she was right, but not knowing the set-up of the final game.

Xxxi

"The object is to enter, make contact with the killer, and then get out," Butterfield told me.

"Easy enough," I said. I was petrified.

"Are you armed?"

"No."

"Good," he said.

I sighed. No weapon.

"Nervous?" he asked.

"No." I wanted to run.

I was shaking.

"You know, I'm sorry about all this," he said.

I walked out of the grocery, towards the cabinetmakers and passed policeman Foley. He was in plain clothes and police boots.

He ignored me.

I entered the cabinetmaker's door, but no one was there. I stood inside the doorway. My senses, peaked.

The main room of the ground floor was large and cluttered with towers of unstained drawers and dressers stacked two-high. The smell of sawdust and resin overpowered the entire space. In the next room, there was more unfinished clutter. Hammers hung from holsters nailed along the edge of a long workbench. A few were empty.

"Up here!" I heard a man yell from the first floor. "Help! I'm up here."

The plea made me shudder, but after a moment, propelled me to act.

I found the staircase at the back of the showroom and cautiously looked up it to see if I could spot anyone. All I saw were cedar rafters and cobwebs. I resisted the urge to run up the stairs, to instead wait out a possible ambush. My heart was racing and I felt like my heartbeat could be heard by my killer. Breath, I told myself. Fucking breath.

"Is anyone there? Please, he's dead." A man's voice yelled from above.

I couldn't hold any longer and crept up the stairs where I saw Charles and another man tied up and on the ground.

"Enoch!" he screamed. "Untie me, he's coming back."

I felt my anger stir.

"Do you think I'm stupid?" I said.

"What on earth—no, of course not," he said, near crying. "Please untie me. Look what he did to the doctor."

I reluctantly stepped closer to Charles, and beside him, next to a large bubbling pot of glue was the body of Dr. Tom. His face was emulsified within a milky burial mask of hardened glue.

"Colman's mad, Enoch," Charles said. "He put Tom's head into the pot of glue after the doctor told him he wouldn't cover up for him anymore."

"I'm not going to untie you, Charles."

"But it's him!" he said.

I ignored him.

"It wasn't until I figured out you have a brother that it made sense," I said.

"There had to be two of you to make it work."

Charles ignored me.

"Colman, Yesler, Burke, Furth—they've all taken a turn," Charles said.

"This should be good."

"Ms. James," he continued.

"The first victim?" I said.

"She was pregnant with Burke's child. She threatened Burke, said she would go to the Tacoma papers about the affair if he didn't put her up in a house."

"And Mr. Adams, the second?" I asked.

"Worked under Furth at Puget Sound National. He figured out Furth was embezzling money. Got himself killed."

"And the girl in the alley, Sue Edmonds?" I asked. "Did she steal a pen from Colman's desk?"

"No, but her father worked with him on raising funds for the Walla Walla Rail until he caught Edmonds touching his daughter. She was an accident anyway; Edmonds pulled the girl in front of him when Colman took a shot at him. That's when Colman lost it and killed Edmonds and the rest of the family.

"From the beginning, he was the one who thought the killings should be connected. No one else possessed the faculties to beat their faces in, but he. It was his idea. He enjoyed it."

"Why?" I asked.

"Control."

"Of what?"

"Seattle. The population," he said. "Stir up fear, drum up a scenario like in London with the Ripper. The people will be too preoccupied and scared to disagree."

"Disagree with what?"

Charles turned away.

"Pity we were never able to work together on the water works project."

"I'm listening," I said.

"It's Furth's water works company, but Colman's money."

"So, what're you implying?"

"It's a complicated project," he said. "Colman wasn't happy with the projected time and cost to complete. Once Mayor Morran[lxx] pulled his backing from Springhill for a publicly owned water system, things got desperate. Morran owes his seat to them, but he reneged on their agreement; I'm surprised he's not dead too."

I stepped closer to him.

"You'll have to do better, Charles. What about Richards?"

"Were you aware Winston Cain of the Northern Pacific[lxxi]came to town?"

The lamb roast, I thought.

"What's the significance?" I said.

"He was on his way to Tacoma, via San Francisco to close a deal with Charles Barstow Wright,[lxxii]who worked with the Northern Pacific to lay track to the West Coast. He was an old friend of Colman's, and Colman persuaded Cain to stop into town. They wined and dined him, but Cain laughed in Colman's face when Colman asked him to put the NP's interest in Tacoma's rail expansion on hold until the Seattle City Council unveiled their plan for a renewal project. And, well, then it happened."

"What happened?"

"He shot him, right there where he stood, next to Yesler, Burke and myself."

"What were you doing there?"

"Burke invited me along for the dinner. Furth was there too. I'm the one who'd gone through the legal and the city maps."

"No, no, Colman can't be the killer," I said.

Pounding came from downstairs. I ran to them and was afraid I would be in harm's way, so I stopped and turned back to Charles."

"Is he your brother?" I asked.

"Who?"

"Don't be daft. Policeman Foley."

"Yes."

"Did he tell you about what's going on here?"

"I haven't spoken to him," Charles said. "Colman's kept me here since last night."

I thought back to the night outside Yesler's Wharf.

"Why in the hell did he kill Dr. Tom?" I said.

"When Colman lured me up here to check on some matter to do with the sewage system, the doctor was already up here and looked like he'd been for a while." Charles' face twisted. "He's tying off his loose ends."

The pounding continued and I braved it and ran to the lip of the stairs.

Two officers were pounding in nails to seal off the front door. I was confused. Desperate. I didn't know who to trust. I ran downstairs and pounded on the door, but the officers (who devil would have it were the same two I'd seen before, tailing Mr. Richards) paid no attention and sealed me in. Things were not going in the direction I expected. I grabbed a hammer from the shop and ran back upstairs.

"What about the bar massacre they blamed on Robert? Colman couldn't have made easy work of that group."

"The Indian could have," he said.

"No, not a chance."

"It wasn't Colman, I know that much," he said.

"There's no motive."

"I couldn't tell you, but from what I've heard passed on between the Council, it was a lucky strike."

"Again, I don't buy it," I said.

"You don't have to."

"Explain the letters. I suppose they were manufactured?"

"I wrote them myself," Charles said.

He relaxed his shoulders and a change washed over him—a sickly confidence akin to a martyr soaked in petrol. I played along.

"Bollocks," I said.

"You saw way too much too soon," he said. "For God's sake, the night you came into town you passed Colman in the alley right after they planted Ms. James' body."

"Planted?"

"Colman's victims were shot first—you failed to ever notice because you were too busy looking at their faces. Dr. Tom was in on it, so he never exposed the wounds. That's why he's dead."

"And who cut off my hand?"

"Glad you asked," he smiled. "My brother of course. Colman was sure you identified him and was so paranoid about it he persuaded Butterfield to get you killed."

His story was growing thin.

"I'm sorry, but your brother comes across as pretty slow in the head. Definitely not the man I spoke with."

"You think he'd drop any hint to spark your memory."

"But the typewritten letter? It was obviously a mistake," I said.

"A double-blind. Butterfield said you lied to him about the letters being typed the night Colman killed the little girl and the rest of the Edmonds family. Why don't you think you were ever pressed about turning in the letters until McGilvra returned to Seattle?"

"Because they were inconsequential," I said.

"Evidence belonging to a set-up?" he snickered. "They only started pressing you about them to double you up. They wanted to see if you thought they were guilty of any wrongdoing and how you'd react. Colman actually is the one who flipped and wanted you alive, but after his show at the wharf, he's not calling the shots anymore."

"What do you mean?"

"Yesler wants his head on a platter," he said. "Covering up Cain's murder was the last straw; it put everyone in jeopardy, and the plan."

"What you mentioned before, the waterworks?" I said.

Glass broke downstairs. Then more.

"The plan."

"But why Anna?" I said.

"The whore? Lou thought she might have picked up on something. She was Richard's favorite, you know?"

I held back my anger.

"Richards was in on the plan?"

The smell from the glue pot intensified. Charles looked away from me, distracted by whatever was coming up the stairs. I felt panic. I needed to sort out who did what, but I'd never know.

"Smoke!" he cried. "Untie me."

Smoke seeped through the floorboards.

"Richards!" I yelled to regain his attention.

"They're setting the building on fire!" he said.

"I can see."

"Richards was never involved, but knew Colman was up to something and wanted in. He had his own ties to San Francisco money and knew between Colman and Furth's banking connections, there was money to make. He stumbled onto Cain's corpse and that sealed his fate. Sealed Anna's too. There was no way anyone from outside the circle could live. Funny thing is, you were there, weren't you? He told them, but as you can imagine, you were off limits."

"But I'm nothing and Colman was going to kill me anyway," I said.

"You are nothing, Enoch, but your father's fortune means a great deal. Obviously, it was a mistake on Colman's part to want you dead, but when your father's letter came in, accepting an invitation to invest in rebuilding Seattle and a massive check, you had to stay alive. The whole conspiracy hinged on his investment."

"So, this was all about burning down the city?" I said. "Or, in your case, stopping it?"

The floor creaked from behind and I turned. It was officer Foley.

"Two days in a week that I'll be knocking you out," he said.

Before I could react, I fell with thunder in my ears.

Xxxii

Charles pulled me up by my hair and dragged me through a small door on the other side of the glue pot. He was perspiring and roughed up. Dr. Tom's wax-figured face ripped past my vision and then all was dark.

"We need to get out of here," I said.

"Shut up," he returned.

I heard him kick against a wall until a sliver of light gave through. He kicked again and a breach in the wall exposed another section of the old building. He threw my head though it and I tumbled onto a pad caked in pigeon shit. The heat from under the loft floor was hot, and I tried to pick myself up from it, but my arm couldn't support it.

"My bastard double crossing brother," he said.

"Your accomplice," I said.

"Come on!"

He grabbed me by the collar and pushed me through a door and we entered a hallway of office doors. We started down it and came to the end and descended the ground level stairs, but they were engulfed in flames. The smoke was thick like a fist down my throat, and I could barely turn back up the stairs because I was retching. We went up another flight, to the top level.

"Shut up," Charles said and opened the first door he came across and threw me in.

"Don't go anywhere," he ordered. "I'll find a way out."

I looked around and the window was nailed shut from the outside. Below I saw a crowd gathering outside the building. It was the same crowd as when the boy drowned in the sinkhole. I was trapped. I didn't know what to do; I couldn't stand without the room spinning. I sat down and stared stupid out the door and watched the smoke from downstairs crawl up the walls. What Charles told me agreed with what I already figured out about the Council's plot to damage the city, but in so doing, counterintuitively proved to me he was the killer. They were all guilty of something, but the greatest thing I couldn't reconcile was how the insipid Charles suddenly became so powerful and ornery? I couldn't let him win. He returned to the room.

"Come on!" he yelled.

"No," I said. "I can't move."

"Come on, there's a way."

"It doesn't matter; even if we get out we'll never live," I said.

He ran over to me, grabbed my handless wrist and squeezed it as hard as he could. His eyes were alight with fury and hatred. I was awake. The pain erupted up through my arm, and I lunged at him, knocking him to the floor. I'd snapped and began to beat him in the face with my good fist and he laid there without defending himself. "What about stopping this?" I said, straddling him and continuing to punch him. "Aren't we supposed to stop history together?" I gave him a shot to the kidney and grabbed hold of his throat. "You mean to tell me you just watched it all happen—you watched Colman and the rest plot to destroy the city, and did nothing?"

"Nothing!" he screamed. "You call my efforts to save you, nothing!"

He pushed me off and attempted to kick my side, but I lunged at him and wrestled him into submission. With his belly on the hot floor— wisps of smoke rose from the wooden floorboards—he tried to wiggle himself free.

"Why the hell did you need me?" I said. "Were you too weak to go through with the killings yourself?"

He began to laugh and spat blood on the floor. It ran like hot oil.

"Who's this?" he said. "This couldn't be Enoch, the tortured soul? Couldn't be."

"Well, you've failed to stop time," I said, flipping him over. "Looks like the city will burn despite your efforts." I popped him in the nose and blood began to gush out.

He wallowed for a moment and then again tried to laugh it off.

"I didn't kill for nothing," he smiled, blood settling in between his teeth. "You needed motivation, and I needed to make those bastards responsible for their greed, even if I couldn't save the city."

I looked at Charles, the killer, and for the first time saw how weak he was. Not his body, but his mind.

"My only mistakes were thinking I could scare the City Council, and get you to convince your father to pull his investment. "

"So that's it," I said. "Scare me out of town and convince my father there's no investment here. Pathetic plan."

"I was also like you, bored," he said.

"So kill innocents?" I said. "Kill a little girl? Kill Anna, frame the Council and Robert? Your philosophy and theories have undone us all, including yourself."

"The logic is sound," he said.

"What about right and wrong?"

Smoke filled the room and our conversation would have to wait. I yanked the bloody philosopher from the scalding floorboards and dragged him by the hair to the adjacent room where there was a shattered bay window. I pushed him to the sill and scanned the crowd below.

"We're brothers now," he said.

I felt a sharp pain creep into the muscular wall of my side. I looked down and there rested the wooden handle of a knife. I grabbed Charles by his collar and threw him headlong out the window and watched him fall. I saw the crowd catch him. I raised my eyes to the blue sky turning black with smoke; it changed and gave way to an endless dark ocean. I felt a hand on my shoulder and a draft of warm breath caress my neck. A push sent me out of the window. I was falling, with no wings to save me, but the mob caught me. I was flipped around and settled onto the ground. There above, standing in the broken window, was the little girl in the white dress holding Flora's hand. Not a fly to be seen around Flora. No black mass spewing from her mouth. Just her. I don't remember anymore besides the faces of the crowd staring down at me. Each different and unique. Not a single throw-away among them.

Xyxii

The fire engine took too long to be carted up the hill, and once it arrived, proved ineffective. The hydrant's water pressure was so low it would've been more effective to round up all the drunks in town and have them collectively piss on the blaze.[lxxiii] The city burned. The fire tumbled south. Morran ordered Colman's prized office building blown up to contain the fire's advancement. It didn't work. The fire skipped over the rubble and swallowed Skid Road and the Lava Beds. It ate the city's hotels, Seattle's precious opera house, and Lou's brothel. All the taverns, the workhouses, and even Yesler's mill were reduced to piles of smoldering ash. Skid Road was finally cleansed, and every festering mattress in the Lava Beds, incinerated. The wharf sizzled with the lap of the tide, and plumes of smoke mixed with the sea air, sending sinewy ghosts up the avenues coughing salt upon the wreckages. Seattle looked like hell if hell could ever stop burning. I survived.

I was startled awake by another one of Morran's explosions and found myself surrounded by the scissoring legs of a crowd who'd lost interest in me. They followed the boom south to catch up with the blaze. Its charred trail consumed the street signs rendering the city a nameless disaster. I struggled to my feet, the stab wound to my side, bandaged, the knife, gone. I walked with everyone else—the mob—but much slower, and without the wonder and excitement that enraptured the rest. I had stepped into one of my dreams, not a nightmare, and not at all coded in Furth's mystery of the subconscious. The meaning of what I saw was deliberate and obvious: No one will ever unearth the longhouse. It will stay quiet, safely submerged in Elliott Bay. Seattle will continue to destroy itself a hundred times over to find it until it too slips into the sound. Progress cannot defy the natural consequence of beginning; it must also end.

Burke saw me and ran my way.

"My god, Enoch!" he said. "You're alive."

He looked glossy and heavenly for a liar, and though it occurred to me to strike him, I was too unsteady to even attempt it.

"I was stabbed," is what came from my mouth.

"What happened inside the cabinet makers?"

I kept walking and he followed.

"Enoch?"

"I don't bloody know," I said.

He stopped.

"I'll get you help," he said, and I presume left to do so.

The sky was black, but cut open with glass fragments of blue sky every time the wind came up. Hands grasped my arms. It was Burke and Furth.

"Good god, Enoch," Furth started. "We thought you were dead. No one escaped from our side of the building. We heard a man jumped, but we figured it was Charles. You were supposed to come out with one of Butterfield's men."

"Foley?" I said. "He was in on it. I woke up on the street."

Lou ran up and embraced me.

"Like hell you didn't run. One of the girls said she saw you running like wild as soon as the crowd got you onto your feet."

"I don't remember," I said.

She looked at my eyes.

"He's not all there," she said. "Enoch—"

"Leave me alone," I said.

They all froze.

"Enoch, you've been injured," Furth said.

Colman saw us from the corner and ran up.

"Enoch, my boy, you're all right."

The bar broke. I couldn't take it. I leapt at him and kissed my forehead against his chin. He fell, and I on top of him.

"You set me up, set me up to die in there."

Furth and Burke pulled me off, and I swung loose from them.

"What on earth are you talking about? He's mad," Furth said.

Lou was nursing Colman, who was sitting up on the ground.

"You nailed me into the building because I knew about your plans to burn down the city."

"Enoch, you're not well," Lou said, looking up from Colman.

"You figured if Charles didn't kill me, the flames would. You knew Foley was his accomplice."

I pointed around to the smoking rubble that surrounded us. I lost my balance and fell. Colman stood up and asked Lou to stay with me while he got help. I lost my senses and sat in the middle of the street in a daze. The same people I was convinced tried to have me killed, consoled me.

I settled down after some time and Lou said to me,

"You're safe now. Everything will be alright."

"Charles was the killer," I said.

"We know."

Lou smiled at me and caressed the side of my head.

"You did good," she said.

The coach arrived and Furth and Burke took me to Colman's home because it was north of the cabinet shop and in no danger to catch fire. I was exhausted and let the doctor and Colman guide me into the house without resistance. I was laid onto a bed and left alone. They locked the door. I slept until evening, when the door was unlocked and opened. Colman came in first and then Butterfield.

"You're lucky to be alive," Butterfield said, without much feeling.

I didn't respond.

"I want to know what happened in there."

I was certain it didn't matter what I said, so I began where I found Charles and Dr. Tom's corpse, all the way through the conspiracy, and ended with throwing Charles out of the window. They listened. Colman, especially, was soft in his demeanor.

"Enoch," he said. "It's been too much. The death of Flora, coming to America, and then the murders, and the stress of being a suspect." Colman looked at Butterfield. "You should rest, we can talk in the morning." Colman stepped to the door.

"Where's Charles?" I said.

"We don't know."

Xxxiv

I imagine we would have met in John McGilvra's office, but it burned down so we convened in Colman's dining room. There wasn't the strange butler, just Agnes pouring tea and serving cake. "Post-fire cakes," she joked.

"What of this mischief I hear about you attacking James?" McGilvra jumped straight in.

"John, no," Colman said. "Enoch was in a state of near madness after surviving the fire and being stabbed."

"By Charles, you tell me," McGilvra said.

"That's why I've called you here—along with Butterfield." Butterfield entered on cue. "There's no other way to explain this situation but to first clarify that Charles was in fact the killer and we'd known so. The night before last, when he shot Cain point blank in front of us outside Yesler's Wharf, was the proof."

"Why was he not arrested then?" McGilvra asked, shaken.

"Blackmail."

"What do you mean?

"Just that. And you knew it, John. You probably even put him up to some of it not realizing he was completely insane," Colman said.

"James, I won't tolerate you insinuating that—"

"Enough, John. I know damn well you have a file on every mayor past and present, every councilman and businessman in Seattle, and that's your prerogative. However, Charles used that information to devastating effect."

Butterfield stepped in.

"Enoch, we used you and Charles to bait his accomplice—"

"And to kill us both in the process?"

Colman cleared his throat.

"If you want the truth, then you need to understand the real world, Enoch," he said. "There were too many people fit to suffer if Charles talked. He was dangerous and deserved to be taken down."

"I'm just sorry we didn't know Foley was his brother," Butterfield said.

"What was his role in this mess?"

"He was to make sure you got out of the building and Charles didn't."

"Talk about bad luck," I said.

This didn't explain Dr. Toms' corpse or disposing of Charles earlier.

"Why not kill Charles in a quieter way?"

"It was on the table, but the opportunity presented itself when we captured him."

"So, Richards and Dr. Tom were both sacrificed to bury Cain's murder? You kill Anna too?"

The men eyed each other.

"That was Charles; we didn't know Richards was with her. He was doing his best to confuse you and think we'd manufactured everything. Killing Anna was his way of tipping you over the edge. As for the doctor, he was alive when we left him with Charles."

"But he was to die too, right?"

"Do you have any idea what would happen to the future of Seattle if it went public a Northern Pacific Railroad man was murdered in Seattle amongst the business leaders of the city?"

"But it's wrong."

"Jesus," McGilvra muttered.

"We were lucky we had a drug addict and a sour, good-for-nothing drunk and People's Party[lxxiv] chair to sacrifice, instead of an actual good citizen," Butterfield said.

Colman shuddered at the sound of Butterfield's whiney justification but then said to me:

"To be clear, if you talk to anyone about Cain and the fire, your family will lose everything, maybe even more than money."

"You wouldn't?" I said.

He looked away from me.

"We would," McGilvra said.

"Father invested that much into your scheme?"

"Almost everything," Colman said.

"I have no leverage," I said. "But, what about the murders?"

"What about them?" Butterfield asked.

"Are you charging Charles with them?"

"Charles is long gone."

"Regardless, he's guilty," I said. "So, Robert can go free?"

"The Indian?" McGilvra questioned.

"Not a chance," Butterfield said.

"But you know who the killer is."

"There's no proof Charles killed the four men at the bar."

"It was Officer Foley," I said.

"The point is moot," McGilvra said. "Robert confessed."

"He's innocent."

"We cannot tell the public we were wrong and that the real killer got away," Butterfield said.

"But it's the truth."

"They need justice, not the truth," Colman said. "They've wanted the Indian from the beginning and they shall have him tomorrow."

"You're executing him?"

"Not us, the law," McGilvra said.

"Brilliant," I said. "Just fucking brilliant."

"James, I don't like this boy's attitude," said McGilvra.

"I couldn't give a bollocks—the lot of you."

They were silent so I continued.

"You're all corrupt and responsible for at least the murders of Cain, Richards and the doctor. You also sunk Cain's boat. If my father's name and wealth were not on the line I would—"

"Have us arrested?" McGilvra said.

Colman looked down to his lap and Butterfield snorted and grinned. I realized I couldn't do anything. I felt weak. A fraud.

"I'm not going to say anything," I said. "How can I? If it were my life, I'd sacrifice it, but I can't ruin my family. I want to leave this place, can it be arranged?"

"Certainly," Colman said. "Where?"

"Anywhere. California."

"Anything else."

"The typed letter I was sent."

"That was a miscommunication between Furth and Burke. We voted against sending it to you, but it was sent anyway. Charles delivered it without our knowing," Colman said.

"And you had Foley retrieve it?"

"Burke pleaded with me," Butterfield said. "Foley volunteered. Volunteered to be the one inside the cabinetmakers' too."

"Did he burn up in the cabinet shop?" I said.

"We think he got out."

"I wouldn't be too sure about that," I said.

I smiled—I remembered.

"What are you smiling at, boy?" Butterfield said.

"Progress."

Xxxv

The city was jovial. Furth pledged unlimited support through his bank for the rebuilding of Seattle. Millions of tons of stone had already been quarried, and Colman's trains were ready to roll them in. Yesler made plans for his new dream home. Seattle was to be rebuilt in fire-safe stone and its plumbing, cast-iron piping. Their only sacrifice, turning over Springhill Water Company to the people. With the new publicly owned water system, the entire downtown area was to be raised anywhere from 14 to 22 feet to prevent flooding and pressure inconsistencies within the pipes due to the tides. Most of the men on the City Council, including other successful names in the city, like Denny, Boren and Maynard, owned the majority of the land. They stood to gain once they could raise their buildings and have Seattle look like a real city.

I heard later a burned out boat surfaced near Colman's new dock and he had the vessel towed and buried inside the foundation of his new office building. Colman told my father it was to save time and money. My father had a good laugh at Colman's frugality, but I couldn't muster a smile.[lxxv] I eventually made it back to Scotland after a tour through the corners of America. I found it hard to enjoy my travels because of the murders. On the sail back to Scotland I came to an understanding about my life and my purpose. Through escaping death, or rather, watching it destroy me in the Northwest region of America, I realized I was more than handless, but half-hearted too. Love would never come easy.

• • • • •

I left with a single suitcase and said goodbye to Anges, who was upset by the matter. I walked through the waste that was Seattle and saw Angeline sitting on a crate off the corner where the cabinetmakers building used to stand on Front and Madison. I approached her.

"Good morning, Angeline," I said, but she did not reply. "Is anything the matter?"

"Just go, killer," she said and turned away.

I did just that, because I felt like I was. I killed Robert to save my family.

I was to meet my coach upon the collar of the jog between what was Mill and Front. Robert was to be hanged today in the makeshift police station Butterfield secured further south of town. The people petitioned for it to be public, but the Council agreed that was barbaric and not in line with the values of the new Seattle. The hanging was to happen within half an hour of my ride out of town. The city sat flat and stretched like it'd been abandoned. There was next to nobody on the streets. Small pillows of smoke escaped several of the larger mounds of charred rubble and danced uphill towards the woods.

The thought of leaving was a relief. However, I was still confused about the proceedings of the past couple days and found it impossible to untangle Charles's actions from Colman's and the Council's. I needed some time away from it, and maybe everything would become clear. It never did. The story remained an enigma. Never peace.

·　　·　　·　　·　　·

I passed onto Occidental when I saw a body hanging between two Maple trees in front of what was Yesler's mansion. Two men stood below the body and then hurried away, toward me. They approached shaking their heads is disgust. "You don't want to see it," they said. "Turn around and go to the police station if you want to see a hanging." I nodded but stepped onto Yesler's old property anyway and approached the two charred trees where his prized scantlings were reinstated. There, where years before an angry mob had taken the law into its own hands and strung up two murderous thieves, the burned corpse of Policeman Foley, in uniform, now hanged, face pulverized, a wooden sign hung around his neck by a thick rope:

TOO LATE?
HERE HANGS ROBERT THE INDIAN'S INNOCENCE
THE HANSON SALOON KILLER

Dublin, 1916

Dooley concentrated on the ornate contours of the tin ceiling above him and drew in a slow breath. The sterile hospital air still burned at his throat and lungs, but was tolerable. Three days of rest had done him good. He reached for a glass of water and winced as he completed his task. He took a drink, still tasted like charcoal. He looked over to where he took the glass and decided to hold onto it to avoid the pain of turning his body again. He wasn't sure what he'd done to his body to make the muscles in his chest and back so sore, but he survived a burning room so all was fair play and to be expected. He sat, glass in hand, no nurse, no visitors, and no friends.

He wondered when Cormac's funeral would be and felt guilty because he'd involved his friend in the troubles surrounding Enoch's manuscript. If only he'd thrown it away, he thought. If only he'd taken the hodgepodge of self-aggrandized memories and superfluous meanderings of his fellow countryman and used it to fuel his fireplace perhaps Cormac would still be alive. Inside of his troubled mind, the doctor knew none of this was his fault. If anything, he was trying to get to the bottom of the killings and Cormac was helping do the same. It was impossible to know the killer was tracking him; the killer knew what Enoch sent him; the killer saw an opportunity to make more of the storm he'd already created. There was little Dooley could have done. He felt powerless, like he possessed no control over his safety. The killer was winning, or perhaps, had already won.

"I'll be damned if he has", Dooley said out loud, spilling over his water. A nurse entered right then and gave the doctor a curious smile. She set down some instruments and walked to the foot of his bed.

"Are you alright, doctor?" she said.

"Can you take my glass?"

The glass beside his leg was tipped on its side.

"A new sheet as well?"

Dooley held his gaze out the window and didn't answer. Sunrise.

"I've been told it has been a rough couple days," she said.

"Aye."

She maneuvered to the side of his bed and the growing sun warmed her brown eyes. She put her hand upon his shoulder and peered out the window with him. He turned away, but nodded to acknowledge her kindness. The trees were still dead, he thought, not a single bud yet.

He turned to look at her when a male figure standing in the doorway caught his attention. He wore a brown suit and carried an empty leather satchel.

"Are you going to live?" he asked.

"Excuse me, sir, but who are you?" the nurse asked.

She appeared angry.

"He's my—"

"His brother," Enoch said, interrupting Dooley.

She eyed Enoch suspiciously and then the doctor.

"It's my brother, it's my brother," Dooley said. "I'll go ahead and take the new sheet you promised."

Dooley reassured her with a closed grin and a nod. She sat up and gave Enoch a second eye before sliding past him and out of the room.

The man before Dooley appeared older than he did on the streets when they met below the public hanging off Grafton. He was nearly 50 years-old, yet his face was creaseless, and his eyes, sky blue, red along the edges and wet. He was above average height, underfed, sinewy and fragile at the joints. He wore no smile and didn't appear to possess the ability to.

"Well, here it is," Dooley said.

"Here what is?" Enoch said.

"The bad omen."

Enoch walked closer to the bed, grabbed a chair and sat beside the doctor.

"Do you believe me?"

"I don't know," Dooley said. "My imagination and boredom says yes, but my occupational proclivity to side with rational conclusions says no."

"Perhaps that's the greatest difference between the doctor and a lawyer, one cannot escape the inevitable and enduring truths of science and the other can invent a new reality if the one they're working with isn't justifying their ends."

"Sounds like something your Seattle killer would say," Dooley said.

"Aye, well I was after all the one who was left with the job of paraphrasing his words 27 years after the fact."

"You took many liberties with your manuscript."

"I told it how it felt at the time and how it still feels," Enoch said.

He stood up, set his hat on the seat and walked in front of the window, blocking Dooley's view. Enoch looked like a dark smudge.

"How did you know I was here?"

"I saw the commotion on O'Connell—I've been renting a flat a block away."

"I see. Did you set the fire?"

"No."

"Did you kill Cormac?"

"No."

Dooley snorted and looked away from Enoch and down to his belly. He felt overwhelmed with emotion.

"People just die around me, lad," he said, "they just all slip away." His eyes filled with tears.

Enoch turned to gaze out the window and said nothing.

"The wee brother of the girl they're holding, died," Enoch said. "Is that your fault too?"

"The boy's dead?" Dooley said, wiping his eyes.

"Aye, and it's no one's fault beside the man who killed him."

"And, where on earth do we find him?"

"I don't know, but your man, Joe Plunkett was drawn out of the hospital by his IRB lads. Could barely walk, wonder what that's all about?" Enoch said.

"He's not my lad, he's a patient, and his glands needed to be operated on. As for why he's been removed, I have no idea, but he should be in bed."[lxxvi]

"Something's about to happen in the city," Enoch said.

"Another killing? Comes as little surprise."

Enoch caught sight of the nurse looming near the door and kneeled in close to Dooley.

"No, something bigger," he whispered. "I've heard rumors of German guns. If the likes of Sean MacDermott[lxxvii]and Tom Clarke[lxxviii]pulled Plunkett from his bed, something's going on, and whatever it is, our killer is somehow involved."

"You mean, Charles?"

"If that's his real name, if he's ever had one."

"Are we to stop the IRB now?" Dooley said.

"We just wait and see what happens—Charles will turn up when he wants."

"No, this is for the RIC to deal with."

"That's what Charles wants. Think of all the ways you're connected to the killings. You visited Ashling, Cormac was killed after your meeting, and we were present at the last killing, where witnesses can place us."

"That he set fire to my flat surely places me as a victim?"

"Or, a guilty man trying to misplace the blame," Enoch said. "I wouldn't be surprised if he planted something in your flat for the RIC to find."

Enoch looked up and caught the nurse coming at him with a scalpel. He grabbed his chair, losing his hat, and held it between them.

"You bastards, bleeding killers, you killed my babies!" she screamed, slashing at the chair.

Dooley scrambled off the bed and to his feet, the pain in his body secondary to his fear.

"We've done no such thing," said Dooley.

She clenched her teeth and wheezed as if a wild beast.

"He promised me he would find the men who killed my husband

and took my girl," she said, panting and losing control of her breathing. "He told me you'd meet here after the fire. He told me I could find you here… kill you here."

The nurse's eyes went blank and her body relaxed. She buried the blade deep inside her neck and yanked it across without a shudder. Her eyes looked past the two men like staring out onto the ocean, a sea of blood rushed from her carotid. The men looked upon the young mother in horror. She fell to the ground and gurgled for breath, her hands clasped in prayer over her artery. Enoch attempted to seal the wound with his hand, but the doctor stopped him. "What's that there?" He pointed to an envelope sticking out from the nurse's apron. Enoch grabbed it.

"We need to leave right now," he said.

The doctor was paralyzed.

"Doctor, let's go."

Enoch grabbed the doctor and pulled him to a wheelchair stationed in the corner. He peaked out the door, the hallway was empty. He shut the door behind them and wheeled the doctor down the hall.

"Why are we leaving?" Dooley said.

"I haven't been completely truthful."

"I knew I should've thrown your manuscript into the fireplace!"

"Open the letter," Enoch said, ignoring Dooley and handing him the envelope.

The doctor opened it and inside was a business card.

> *Charles Jozef Bertrand*
> *Psychiatrist and hypnotist*
> *15 Mary Street*

"There's something written on the back," Dooley said, watching ahead to make sure Enoch didn't run his legs into anything as they hurried down the hall.

"What does it read?"

The doctor held the card up in front of Enoch's face.

"Gentleman, your first victim," Enoch read aloud.

He clenched his teeth, quickened his pace, and pushed the wheelchair on a crash course for the exit.

"Why are we running?" Dooley shouted.

The wheelchair burst through the exit and onto the footpath.

It was early Monday morning, April 24th, 1916.

Something was amiss.

Endnotes

---

[i] Madame Lou Graham (1857-1903): Dorothea Georgine Emile Ohben arrived in Seattle in February 1888, and shortly after opened the most popular bordello in Seattle. Businessmen, dignitaries, and the powerful elite all frequented her establishment, and her success coined her the title: Queen of the Lava Beds (the red-light district of old Seattle). Lou was feared and hated by most because of her stranglehold on the "seamstress" market and her intimate knowledge of her many patrons' indiscretions. She often supplied under the table loans to businessmen at higher interest rates, and during the financial crisis of 1893, made a killing doing just that. The site of her hotel is now occupied by the Union Gospel Mission. Madame Lou died of syphilis at 42.

[ii] Oddfellows building: Many believe the original Oddfellows Hall is located on Capitol Hill, on Pine Street and 10th Avenue, but this is not the case. The original hall was located on Front Street and Columbia. I believe there was an alleyway behind the building, but I cannot be positive. Regardless, I created an alley as I needed one to lay a body in. The point is rather moot at this point as it has all burned to the ground and been buried over by new buildings.

[iii] Henry Yesler (1810?-1892): William C. Speidel wrote of Yesler in his book, *Sons of the Profits* (1967) Yesler, "...never willingly paid his just debts. He cheated his friends until he ended with none. He utilized public office for private gain. He drove more wealth out of King County than he ever brought in. The City of Seattle made him a millionaire, yet he sued it... fought it... plundered it... and on two occasions he brought it to the brink of bankruptcy." Henry Yesler started the Yesler Mill on Mill Street. Mill Street is today Yesler Way. Businessman, and a two-time former mayor, Yesler had his hands in about everything and every pocket. I'll add, I spent my teenage years living in the Yesler Terraces (Central District) and the bulk of its occupants felt the same about the City Council as Speidel felt about Henry Yesler. The Yesler Terraces were torn down in 2016-2017.

[iv] Thomas Burke (1841-1925): Described by some as a "professional beggar" because of his ability to raise private funds for major city works and construction, Burke was a gifted lawyer who made partner with John McGilvra, his father in-law. Known as a fair lawyer and Judge, Burke was also called out by his biographer, Robert Nesbit as someone "not inclined to unprofitable idealism." He's characterized in the following pages as a bit of a groveler, but I have little knowledge of what he was really like. I needed a tag-along character to round-out my cast of social elites, and he seemed as good a candidate as any.

[v] John McGilvra (1827-1903): Former US attorney general and friend of Abe Lincoln, McGilvra was brought to Seattle by the prospect of the railroad. He founded the Seattle Bar Association and used his law firm and connections to make a lot of money, notably investing on public transit projects like the Madison Street cable car system. He was of Scottish ancestry, but was quite removed from the motherland, as his family immigrated before the Revolutionary War. Still, I'm sure he was told a story or two about Scotland's past, he at least says so in this book.

[vi] Chinese riots: February 6th-9th 1886. Anti-Chinese resentment and fanaticism in Seattle reached its apex in 1886, and culminated in a round-up of virtually every Chinese resident in Seattle. They were forced onto a dock to board a boat for San Francisco. 200 boarded the vessel and 150 were stranded until the next boat was meant to disembark 6 days later. When the remainder were directed to return to their homes by city officials, the anti-Chinese mob comprised mainly of working-class whites, Socialist firebrands, and Utopianists, rioted. Shots were fired into the crowd and one agitator was killed.

[vii] Yesler's scantlings: The scantlings were made famous in the 1882 mob lynching of James Sullivan and William Howard for the robbery and murder of businessman, George B. Reynolds. Benjamin Payne, the prime suspect in the murder of a policeman, David Sires, was also strung up by the mob. Yesler found this incident to be an exemplary model of justice and left the scantlings up in his trees as a reminder of the event. He was quoted: "That was the first fruit them trees ever bore, but it was the finest." There, the scantlings remained for 7 years until they were stolen days before the Great Fire of 1889.

[viii] Railroad terminus: The terminus was actually allocated by the Northern Pacific to Tacoma on July 14th, 1873. However, by 1890 the NP's plan for Tacoma had capitulated to the meows of Seattle's businessmen, politicians, and investors. By 1889, the elite of Seattle most likely knew the change of terminus was waxing into their favor. I created the correlation between the hangings on Yesler's property and Seattle's failure to secure the NP terminus for dramatic affect.

[ix] Yesler's lottery: As with the above note, this is also true. Here's an excerpt from Historylink.com: "On July 4, 1876, the Grand Lottery of Washington winners are supposed to be drawn. Yesler Sawmill, the Seattle establishment that in the early 1850s was the first steam sawmill in Washington, is advertised as the Grand Prize. But then, Henry Yesler, the organizer, cancels the drawing. Yesler kept about 90 percent of the estimated $30,000 ($1,122,000 in 1996 dollars) collected. For this fraud Yesler is assessed a $25 ($935 in 1996 dollars) fine." http://www.historylink.org/File/223 Like many lotteries of the day without proper regulation and oversight, they were predatory games of chance which exploited the poor and working-class's dreams of overnight success and fortune

[x] Seattle Chief of Police, OD Butterfield: Seattle.gov was at least good enough to list O.D. Butterfield's name on their chronological list of police chiefs. Historylink.com has 0 results for him. He's not listed in the index of either Murray Morgan's, *Skid Road*, or William Speidel's, *Sons of the Profits*. Butterfield is as much a peripheral character in Seattle history, as he is in this book. I relied on a cliché when characterizing him as an ineffective and corrupt cop, and I'm sure his true behavior was quite different than how he is written here. Minus the clichés whenever possible, the above statement is applicable for the personalities of every historical actor mentioned in this book. After all, historical fiction is still fiction, even though the breadth of an author's research may try and confuse this fact. Also, as this is an admitted work of low-brow historical fiction, I did away with endnotes. You're welcome.

[xi] Maximillian Robespierre (158-1794): Influential figure of the French Revolution and Reign of Terror. He began his political career as an opponent of the death penalty, but upon his appointment to the Committee of Public Safety, became a legislator of mass execution to, in his mind, propel the revolution forward. He himself met his end upon the razor's edge of the guillotine, but not before failing to put a bullet through his head, and shooting his jaw off instead. Purity is a funny business.

[xii] Skid Road: Freshly cut logs were skidded downhill to Yesler's saw mill on an acute grad that was then Mill Street, and today known as Yesler Way. Mill Street was the red carpet into the Lava Beds. The term exists in the American urban lexicon to refer to the part of town where the down-and-outs and homeless, the junkies, prostitutes, and pimps, and the mentally ill, reside. Over the years, much has changed in Seattle, but this location remains more or less a graveyard for hope and home to the city and county courthouses.

[xiii] Lava Beds: Red-light district to Pioneer Square first made famous in the mid to late 1800's with the popular brothel, the Illahee, which in Chinook Jargon translates to "home", "country", or "place."

[xiv] Fire Station: Seattle's fire department was solely a volunteer force in 1889. When the city created a full-time fire department the entire lot of volunteers quit. There was no pride in getting paid, especially by an ungrateful city who partially laid the blame on them for failing to put out the Great Fire.

[xv] St. Charles Hotel: My research pointed me to this hotel, although I was unable to find much information about it besides the fact when the original edifice burned down, it was quickly rebuilt with fire-proof brick. The hotel still stands with the same name. I imagined the original building to be quite beautiful and exquisite on the inside. I wanted to imagine it that way while this chase scene was underway in my head.

[xvi] The Throat: A cross streets off of Mill Street (Yesler Way) where the angle of the

street grid changed. Apparently, it was a dicey stretch to cross at certain times of day.

xvii Brunswick Hotel: The original hotel burned to the ground in 1889. It was rebuilt in 1890 and renamed The Dillard Hotel. It's still there and located on 1st Street and University.

xviii Gallus: Commonly used in the west of Scotland to describe an act of boldness or daring.

xix Langston Livery Stable: Popular livery stable that burned down in 1889. A photograph of its façade was featured in Paul Dorpat's Seattle Times, *Now and Then* Column.

xx O'Connell Street: Named after The Emancipator, Daniel O'Connell (1775-1847). Succeeded in his fight for Catholic Emancipation in Ireland and fought against the Act of Union between Britain and Ireland.

xxi General Post Office, 1916: The post office was the central point of armed rebellion by Irish Republicans in an attempt for independence from British rule. The Easter Rebellion, as it came to be called, took place April 24-29th 1916 in Dublin, Ireland. The rebellion failed and its governing members were executed. The event sparked an escalation in violence which eventually lead to the independence of 26 of the island nation's 32 counties in 1922. The Dublin sections of this novel take place in the days leading up to the rebellion. The patricides Dr. Dooley is investigating are fictional.

xxii Temple Bar: Section of central Dublin on the South side of the River Liffey.

xxiii Unionists: Pro Union followers believed in a united Britain and were staunchly against the emancipation of Ireland.

xxiv The Liberties: An area of southwest central Dublin that contained pockets of profound and dire poverty. Most of the area was improved by the mid 20th Century.

xxv Joseph Mary Plunkett (1887-1916): A Dublin born nationalist and writer who helped plan the 1916 Easter Rebellion and was executed days after the surrender of the General Post Office. Plunkett contracted tuberculosis at a young age and spent most of his life physically ailed by his disease. Plunkett underwent neck surgery days before the rebellion and was bedridden for most of the rebellion. Seven hours before he was executed by firing squad, he married Grace Gifford in a small chapel within Kilmainham Gaol.

xxvi Royal Irish Academy (Acadamh Ríoga na hÉireann): Established in 1785 the RIA is an independent forum of peer elected experts who lead, facilitate and make significant contributions to public debate and policy formation in the areas of science, technology, and culture.

xxvii Old Parliament Building: When Ireland was stripped of its own parliament in 1800 the Parliament building ceased to function as Ireland's central house of rule and law. It was eventually purchased by the Bank of Ireland, and in 1916 was still an active bank. The building is located across the street from Trinity College Dublin on College Green, in the center, excuse me, centre of the city.

xxviii Arthur Denny (1822-1899): One of the Founders of Seattle. Supposedly, a pretty likable guy and therefore not featured in this novel.

xxix Doc Maynard (1808-1873): Another founder of Seattle. A friend of indigenous peoples and fine liquor in a time of manifest destiny and the temperance movement.

xxx Bonnie Prince Charlie (1720-1788): Charles Edward Stuart was heir to the throne of the disposed Stuart kings of England and Scotland. Known as the Young Pretender, he followed in his father's footsteps in a failed attempt to overthrow the Hanoverian dynasty, and restore the Stuarts to the English monarchy. In what is known today as the 1745 Rebellion (or simply, the '45) He famously led an army of Highlanders south into England after defeating Hanoverian forces in the Battle of Prestonpans. Marching into England, he begrudgingly took the advice of his generals and turned back into Scotland, where soon after his forces were badly beaten at the Battle of Culloden. He escaped Scotland, but the Highland gentry sympathetic to the Stuart cause (Jacobites) were stripped of their land and wealth, and many were executed for their part in the insurrection. The Highland clearances ensued, removing Highland peoples from their ancestral lands, and forcing them into lowland cities. At the time, this was looked at by many Englishmen and Lowland loyalists to the crown as essential to thwart any future attempts of insurrection, and a measure to force the backward people of the Highlands into a more progressive way of life. Many within the herding and cotter classes of the Highlands were looked at as primitives and savages who were in need of a push to catch up with the times. See footnote lxvii for more on 18th Century views of historical progress, in particular Adam Smith's 4-Stage theory of historical progress.

xxxi Wahalchoo story: Much of this novel's research on native peoples who belong to the geographical area known today as Seattle came from the book *Native Seattle: Histories from the Crossing-Over Place*. Historian, Coll Thrush's examination of NW native peoples' pervasive existence in the evolution of Seattle is profoundly solid in its attempt to break the false master narrative that indigenous peoples belong to a dying culture/race. Instead, Cull shows how Indigenous people are inextricably linked to the history and development of Seattle. In this novel, the main narrative is built around greed, excess, and murder. The two native characters included in this novel—one invented and the other, historical—are characterized either as powerless to the economic realities of the city, or, as in the case of Kikisoblu (Princess Angeline), willing to only participate economically, but not personally. In other words, she possesses little interest in the interests of Seattle's business elite, or for that matter, being a character within my historical crime novel. During the writing of this book, she wanted little to do with it, and wasn't the least fond of Enoch. I didn't blame her and respected her wishes.

xxxii The antagonist of this novel, and the writer of this letter is indeed following the master narrative of the Native American as a part of a dying race. He has fabricated much to do with Jacob Wahalchoo's life for dramatic affect. Wahalchoo was not survived solely by his dog (if he even had a dog) and was married. He also was one of the few tribal leaders and members who signed the Treaty of Point Elliott (1855). There is also little record to suggest what shape or size of dwelling we had. What is known is as Seattle continued to grow, the native peoples of the area were pushed further to the margins of the city. Little Crossing-over place, the settlement where Wahalchoo resided at the time of his vision, is now buried under the King Street Railway Station on 3rd avenue and Jackson Street. Never trust a killer.

xxxiii City Council: The original Seattle City Council of 1889 included Harry White, John N. Wallingford, Frank A. Twichell, Uriah R. Niesz, George W. Hall, T.E. Jones, David E. Durie, F.J. Burns, Henry F. Phillips. None of these men were mentioned in this novel, or are they referred to as members of the Seattle City Council. Instead, it's assumed the business leaders depicted in the book are. Indeed, Henry Yesler was a former member (1884-85), Robert Morran (1887-88), and Jacob Furth (1885-1888), but in early June of 1889, when this novel takes place, none of these men sat on the council. Other characters, like James Colman, Thomas Burke, and James McGilvra never sat on the council.

xxxiv Vice licenses or vice tax: From its early years on, Seattle had its fair share of prostitution, drinking, and gambling. Though many of Seattle's founding fathers were religious men, it was found the greatest way to multiply the young city's wealth was to tax brothels, and create liquor licenses, and licenses for gambling, which included lotteries. In a city fighting for legitimacy, and in a railway terminus war with Tacoma, taxing the sins and vices of its population exponentially raised its annual income and attracted outsiders to come in and spend their money.

xxxv James Colman (1832-1906): Scottish-born Seattle businessman. Leased Yesler's Mill in 1872 after his mill in Port Orchard burned to the ground. After the Northern Pacific announced Tacoma as the terminus of its NW line in 1873, Colman announced the Seattle & Walla Walla line, a line that would connect Seattle to the Walla Walla railway station. Unbelievably, the line turned a profit and was sold. He also built the Colman Dock and several buildings, one of which is an icon of early post-fire Seattle architecture. The Colman building is located on 811 1st Avenue. Legend has it a sailing vessel is buried underneath the building, which will come into play later in this novel. Colman's creosote plant was located where Union Station is now, next to King Street Station, on Jackson. From the history books, it appears Colman did a lot for the City of Seattle, especially when the future of the city was in doubt. As for this book, I threw his character under the bus on a couple of occasion, but it was for the good of the story. Sorry, James.

[xxxvi] Jack the Ripper: Famous serial killer in London committed at least five murders (known as the "canonical five" between August 31st and November 9th, 1888. The idea to have my killer write letters comes from Jack's famous "from Hell" letter sent to George Lusk of the Whitechapel Vigilance Committee. As the latter's letter came packaged with the remnants of a human kidney, our killer's letters come with a litany of intentional historical inaccuracies, misinterpretations of historical theories, and an eye-rolling sense of self-importance commonly found in the layman conspiracy theorist's agenda to be the only one that's privy to the "real truth(s)" of our age.

[xxxvii] Railroad picnic: In 1874, an all-city work picnic took place to begin the Seattle & Walla Walla Railroad. Many of the public came to the event and showed their support by bringing a dish and a shovel. Everyone was so excited.

[xxxviii] Spring Hill Water Company: Although improvements were made to the Seattle water system, and its systems expanded upon, from 1881-1889 (including a pump station on Lake Washington), the existing system wasn't adequate in terms of general use, and woefully substandard in regard to protecting the mostly wooden city from fire. The system failed to function properly on the day of the Great Seattle Fire.

[xxxix] Kidnapped: Written by Scottish Author, Robert Louis Stevenson and first published in *Young Folks Magazine* in 1886. The date of publication is a little later than when this scene would have taken place, but close enough.

[xl] Olympic Mountain Range: Located on the peninsula of Washington State. The east side of the range is visible to Seattle from across the Puget Sound.

[xli] The Brothers: Double-peaked mountain in the Olympic mountain chain, visible from Seattle.

[xlii] Erected by Reverend David Blaine, Seattle's first house of worship, the Little White Church was located on 2nd Avenue and Columbia.

[xliii] Kikisoblu aka Princess Angeline (1820-1896): Kikisoblu was the daughter of Chief Seeathl's, aka Chief Seattle. She lived in a shanty on the north end of the city's waterfront. Doc Maynard's second wife, Catherine Broshears Maynard, created the Princess Angeline moniker. Kikisoblu was with her father when the Denny party settled on Alki Point, and oversaw the drastic transformation of Seattle's geography and population. She was respected by many, but taunted by more. She never took handouts and worked until the day she died. She was buried in a canoe-shaped casket in Lakeview Cemetery.

[xliv] Indian Jargon: As told in Thrush's *Native Seattle*, a man by the name of Ling Fu was in danger of deportation because he had no papers. He argued he was born in the area. When the judge asked him a question in Chinook jargon—a language only a person born and raised in the area could understand and possibly speak—Ling Fu

answered in kind, which satisfied the judge enough he immediately dismissed the case and sent Ling Fu on his way (64).

xlv A chemist is a pharmacist.

xlvi Jacob Furth (1840-1914): Born in Bohemia (today, Czech Republic), Furth was a successful Seattle banker, entrepreneur, and public servant. He was a major supporter of public works and mass transportation schemes, and part owner of the Springhill Water Company. He invested heavily in the growth of Seattle, especially following the Great Fire. He was also an ally and friend to Madame Lou Graham.

xlvii Georg Wilhelm Friedrich Hegel (1770-1831): German philosopher associated with absolute idealism, the master-slave dialectic, and the principle of "spirit" within historical progress. Hegel didn't think of God as an indifferent mover and beyond human history, but God as historical progress itself.

xlviii Sigmund Freud (1856-1936): Father of psychoanalysis, Freud believed a mentally troubled patient could be "cured" by excavating and resolving the repressed conflicts within the subconscious. In his early practice, he used hypnosis as a tool, but gradually did away with the practice in favor of what he called, the "talking cure." In this practice, the patient was encouraged to talk without forethought, in a free associative manner to unlock the deepest traumas and truths buried deep within their subconscious psyche. I'm not sure how much Furth could have actually known about Freud in 1889, even if he wanted to, but nonetheless I went for it. "Sometimes a cigar is just a cigar" is one of Freud's better quotes.

xlix St. Brendan's Hospital: Psychiatric facility located in the North Dublin suburb of Grangegorman. The original structures of the hospital are torn down or in ruins.

l John O'Connor Donelan: Medical Superintendent of St. Brendan's Hospital between 1908 and 1937.

li Ben Lomond: Mountain north of Glasgow located at the foot of Loch Lomond. It's doubtful from Enoch's central Glasgow location on Byres Road he could have seen the mountain, but I made it so.

lii Highland caterans: A Highland band of marauders, professional thieves, and/or mercenaries.

liii Rob Roy MacGregor (1671-1734): A Scottish outlaw and folk hero. A traditional Jacobite, MacGregor was pro-Stuart and Catholic. He was also a cattle herder, and engaged in blackmail to protect people's herds from theft, sometimes from his own theft.

liv Feud with the Duke of Montrose: After losing his lands he (MacGregor) waged a blood feud against his dispossessor, James Graham, 1st Duke of Montrose. The tales that follow include a series of adventures where Rob Roy escapes capture and execution. Bloody brilliant!

^{lv} Scottish rebellions of 1715 and 1745: The 45' explained earlier (note: xxviii) both were failed uprisings to reinstall the Catholic Stuarts to the English monarchy.

^{lvi} The Act of Union 1707: At this time, England and Scotland were two separate states, each with their own parliaments, but under one monarch. Following the War of the Three Kingdoms (1639-1651) and the Glorious Revolution (1688), which saw the overthrow of the Scottish Stuart Dynasty from the English throne, the new Protestant English monarchy increased its effort to consolidate power on the isles. Scotland, politically fractured and near economic collapse, was forced into union in order to open England's colonial markets for trade. The Act of Union expanded English control in Scotland at a time when Scotland was looked at as a threat, and physically speaking, a harbor for England's continental enemies to exploit, namely the French.

^{lvii} Malt Tax Riots: Began on June 23rd, 1725 in retaliation to the imposition of the English malt tax. As the economic promises of the 1707 Act of Union had yet to materialize, Scottish citizens took to the streets in protest and openly riot. The fiercest riots and anti-English sentiment existed in Glasgow.

^{lviii} Kwak'wala: Indigenous language spoken by the Kwakwaka'wakw of Canada. Kwak'wala belongs to the Wakashan language family.

^{lix} "He walked in heaven and watched the angels fall": In the book of Genesis Enoch is described as having lived 365 years before God took him from earth. However, it's assumed God took him alive, thus Enoch has been described as the one who did not see death. In the Apocryphal books of Enoch, he is described as ascending to heaven alive and being appointed the guardian of the celestial treasures and secrets. Enoch is also seen as the overseer of the archangels.

^{lx} James Hogg (1770-1835): Scottish novelist, essayist and poet. Writer of the profound novel, *The Private Memoirs and Confessions of a Justified Sinner.* The book is split between two narratives, the first by the fictitious editor of the memoirs (a man of science), and the second, the murderous confessions of Robert Wringhim (a religious zealot). Without giving away too much, Hogg was aware of how dogmatic belief undermines the strength of a person's theories and convictions. This goes for religion and science.

^{lxi} 31 Westmoreland Street: Original location of the Irish Times. Directly North of Trinity College Dublin.

^{lxii} Trinity College Dublin: Established in 1592 during the reign of Queen Elizabeth I. Ireland's oldest and most "fancy" university.

^{lxiii} Tin and Shells: What's up with the recurring use of tin cups and shells? I suppose, it's a metaphor, (admittedly, heavy-handed) for finding worth in used and broken objects. It's also an indicator of those ostracized by society, or those who choose to opt-out to the notion that purchasing new things solidifies one's standing in society. Fixing and reusing objects is exceptionally more practical and pragmatic than to continually buy new shit. Many of those who benefit from a purchasing society cannot see this, but to those outside, it's rather obvious.

^{lxiv} According to Thrush, in *Native Seattle* (p.70) a man by the name of Moses lived in the same encampment as Kikisoblu, and was likely the same man who hid his dead son, who had perished from smallpox, in a tree trunk outside of town to avoid being rounded up as part of an epidemic scare.

^{lxv} McGilvra's acceptance of Adam Smith's 4-stage theory of historical progress (stadial history) informs his notion that man began in a hunter-gatherer stage, graduated to a herder stage, before progressing to an agricultural stage, and finally maximizing his potential in the commercial stage of historical progress. Famous in Sir Walter Scott's (1771-1832) historical Scottish novels, is the play between Highlander characters and Lowlander characters whom are socio-historically divided by the former being captive in the herder stage and the latter in the commercial. McGilvra is alluding to the Native American views of retribution and personal justice as "archaic." In a commercial stage of progress the gentleman relinquishes his perceived right to seek blood satisfaction, to the law. This viewpoint was highly encouraged in Europe and the United States to do-away with the sport of dueling as a means of claiming blood satisfaction for an affront to one's honor. Trust your lawyers people.

^{lxvi} The Heart of Midlothian (Sir Walter Scott): Written by Scottish novelist, Sir Walter Scott and published in 1818. Considered by some his finest work of historical fiction. At the time Scott was writing, the novel was a literary form fighting for legitimacy. Scott's evocation of history and nostalgic nationalism was an attempt to make the novel more scholarly when many considered it purely for romantic storytelling—a literary form to be read by aristocratic women inside of their drawing rooms to pass the day with. I had a little fun here writing Anna as passing the day reading Scott inside of a brothel. Sorry, Walter.

^{lxvii} The Minch: is a strait in north-west Scotland which separates the north-west Highlands and the northern Inner Hebrides from Lewis and Harris in the Outer Hebrides.

^{lxviii} Sporran: Traditional to male Highland dress, it's a pouch, often made of leather, that sits at the front of the kilt.

^{lxix} Due to complications with high tide the city's inadequate plumbing, reverse pressure caused water to blow out of a toilet when flushed.

[lxx] Mayor Robert Morran (1857-1943): successful businessman who got his start in politics at a young age. It's said he was catapulted into the mayor's seat after a single stint on the city council because he was backed by the business elite of the city. Whatever the cause, he did a fine job while in office and won two terms.

[lxxi] Winston Cain of the Northern Pacific: Fictional character, friend of Colman's who sailed up to the Puget Sound to close a deal with Wright on behalf of Tacoma and must have been the person who brought Colman the leg of lamb. Imagine that, being thanked for sailing a leg of lamb up the west coast of the US with a bullet?

[lxxii] Charles Barstow Wright (1822-1898): A successful businessman who took an active part in the founding of Tacoma and the city's fight for the Northern Pacific Rail terminus.

[lxxiii] The city's water system was ill equipped to handle the magnitude and spread of the fire. The volunteer department was jeered due to their inability to effectively battle the growing blaze.

[lxxiv] People's Party: Anti-immigrant group in Seattle involved in the Chinese Riots.

[lxxv] Ship buried under the Colman Building: As the legend goes, this is correct. Or maybe, it was the remains of Winston Cain's boat? If Winston Cain existed, of course.

[lxxvi] Joseph Plunkett's removal: Plans for the 1916 Easter Rising were set in motion and Plunkett was removed to take part. However, he spent the duration of the rebellion infirmed and bedridden in the General Post Office.

[lxxvii] Seán Mac Diarmada (MacDermott; 1883-1916): Irish Republican and conspirator who was executed by firing squad days after the Easter Rising inside the grounds of Kilmainham Gaol, Dublin.

[lxxviii] Tom Clarke (1858-1916): Irish Republican and conspirator who was executed by firing squad days after the Easter Rising inside the grounds of Kilmainham Gaol, Dublin.

Acknowledgments

I would like to thank Liam McIlvanney for his Scottish-isms and guidance in the early stages of this project. Sonora Jha for the wonderful job teasing out the mature version of this story from its adolescence. Jesse Montini-Vose for the amazing cover art. The Seattle Room, located in the Central Seattle Library, for their time and dedication; without them, Enoch would never have left Lou's. To my father for his unyielding support—he was there every step of the way. Thanks to Christopher Roth for cleaning up my dialogue attribution. Robert E. Kearns for the writing tips. Mark Baumgarten for the ballgames and being there. *Black Rose Writing* for taking a chance on me. My mother for the love. My brothers and sister for keeping me humble. And Liz, for her unyielding support and honesty. I'm extremely thankful to all those who played a direct or indirect role in the creation of this novel.

About The Author

Josef Alton was born in Seattle, Washington and attended Seattle University, Trinity College Dublin, and the University of Otago, New Zealand. He's published with several publications, including the *Australia Journal of Victorian Studies*, *Seattle Weekly* and *City Arts Magazine*, among others. He currently lives in Seattle and works as a general contractor and author.

For more information, please visit:
http://www.throwawayfaces.com/

Thank you so much for reading one of our **Crime Fiction** novels.
If you enjoyed our book, please check out our recommended title for your
next great read!

Bailey's Law by Meg Lelvis

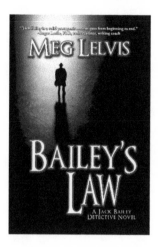

"An intelligent, immersive police procedural that will leave you pining for
another Jack Bailey novel." *—BEST THRILLERS*

View other Black Rose Writing titles at www.blackrosewriting.com/books

and use promo code **PRINT** to receive a **20% discount** when purchasing

CPSIA information can be obtained
at www.ICGtesting.com
Printed in the USA
FFHW021621081218
49767223-54248FF